W9-BTS-469

A secret admirer . . .

"Once I thought that all I had was mine; that what was mine would always be . . ."

Elizabeth froze at the top of the library stairs. *That's from the poem*, she thought, *that's a line from the poem.* Her heart was galloping. She looked around, expecting to see Tom Watts standing behind her.

But it wasn't Tom. If she'd thought about it, she would have known it wasn't Tom. The voice that recited that line didn't belong to him, it belonged to William White. William White, who was standing in the doorway only inches away. He was all in black and holding a white rose in his hand, as though he were a magician just pulling it from the air.

Unable to take her eyes from his, she stumbled for the right words. "I—I don't know what to say," she began. "I mean, thank you. Thank you for everything. For the flowers . . . for the poem . . ."

He touched the rose to her lips. "Thank *you*," he said.

Bantam Books in the Sweet Valley University series
Ask your bookseller for the books you have missed

#1 COLLEGE GIRLS
#2 LOVE, LIES, AND JESSICA WAKEFIELD
#3 WHAT YOUR PARENTS DON'T KNOW . . .
#4 ANYTHING FOR LOVE

Coming soon:

#5 A MARRIED WOMAN

SWEET VALLEY UNIVERSITY™

What Your Parents Don't Know...

Written by
Laurie John

Created by
FRANCINE PASCAL

BANTAM BOOKS
NEW YORK · TORONTO · LONDON · SYDNEY · AUCKLAND

For John Stewart Carmen

RL 6, age 12 and up

WHAT YOUR PARENTS DON'T KNOW ...
A Bantam Book / February 1994

Sweet Valley High® *and Sweet Valley University*™
are trademarks of Francine Pascal
Conceived by Francine Pascal
Produced by Daniel Weiss Associates, Inc.
33 West 17th Street
New York, NY 10011

All rights reserved.
Copyright © 1994 by Francine Pascal.
Cover art copyright © 1994 by Daniel Weiss Associates, Inc.
No part of this book may be reproduced or transmitted
in any form or by any means, electronic or mechanical,
including photocopying, recording, or by any information
storage and retrieval system, without permission in
writing from the publisher.
For information address: Bantam Books

If you purchased this book without a cover you should be aware
that this book is stolen property. It was reported as "unsold and
destroyed" to the publisher and neither the author nor the pub-
lisher has received any payment for this "stripped book."

ISBN: 0-553-56307-6

Published simultaneously in the United States and Canada

Bantam Books are published by Bantam Books, a division of Bantam
Doubleday Dell Publishing Group, Inc. Its trademark, consisting of the
words "Bantam Books" and the portrayal of a rooster, is Registered in
U.S. Patent and Trademark Office and in other countries. Marca
Registrada. Bantam Books, 1540 Broadway, New York, New York 10036.

PRINTED IN THE UNITED STATES OF AMERICA

OPM   0 9 8 7 6

Chapter One

Where is he?

Jessica Wakefield was sitting on her packed trunk, surrounded by cardboard boxes, watching the sunlight spill in through the windows and listening to the ticking of the clock on the wall. Although Jessica had been sharing this apartment with Isabella Ricci since the week after college started, she'd never noticed how angry the ticking of that clock sounded. Angry and sad. She tossed her golden blond hair over her shoulder, kicking the trunk with her heels.

For the first time it struck her how much she was going to miss Isabella and life in the dorm. Since Jessica arrived at Sweet Valley University, the glamorous and sophisticated Isabella had become her best friend and confidante, and living in the dorm had given Jessica the freedom she'd craved but with enough peo-

1

ple always around that she never felt lonely.

Jessica's sea-green eyes traveled around the room. It looked pretty much as it always had—warm, comfortable, and tastefully decorated—but this morning the apartment felt strange and unfamiliar. None of her clothes were draped over the furniture, none of her posters were on the walls. Even her favorite mug, the one shaped like a fish, wasn't on the table half-filled with coffee as it usually was. Everything was packed away. It was as though she were already gone.

"Only, I'm not gone," Jessica sourly informed the empty room. "I'm still here."

Jessica brushed a few strands of hair from her pretty face and sighed. She shouldn't still be here. She should be on the other side of town, helping her boyfriend, Mike McAllery, carry her stuff up to his apartment. They should be laughing and talking and fooling around. They should be standing in his doorway, celebrating the moment of her moving in with him with a long, deep, passionate kiss.

"I'm here and he isn't."

Although she had forbidden them to look again, her eyes moved to the clock. It was eight forty-five.

"Eight forty-five," Jessica announced. "He was supposed to be here half an hour ago." Tick . . . tick . . . tick . . . tick, the clock snarled. "He promised."

This isn't the first time Mike hasn't done what he

2

promised to do, a little voice whispered in her ear. *This isn't the first time he's let you down.*

But Jessica didn't feel like listening to that little voice. It sounded too much like Isabella, her brother, Steven, and her identical twin sister, Elizabeth, three of the many people at Sweet Valley University who disapproved of Mike McAllery.

She got to her feet and went over to the window. There were a few cars in the dorm parking lot, and more hurrying past on the road, but not one of them was a customized, dragon's-blood-red 1964 Corvette.

"Where *is* he?" Jessica asked the window.

"Maybe he's on his way to Mexico," a voice behind her answered.

Jessica turned around to see Isabella coming through the door. "That's not funny, Isabella," Jessica snapped. "Something might have happened. He could have had an accident, or run into my brother and gotten into a fight, or—"

"Found something else to do," Isabella filled in. She threw her books on a chair. "Like he has at least twenty-five times in the last week and a half."

Jessica scowled. "Why do you always have to be so down on Mike?" she demanded. "You'd think that today of all days you could at least be polite."

Isabella's smile was rueful, but not unkind. "I can't be polite about him," she confessed. "I really

3

don't want you to go through with this. You know how unreliable he is. You know he's always putting you off whenever he has something else to do. I thought you'd come to your senses before this."

"I'm doing the right thing, Izz. It'll be different when we're living together," Jessica insisted, as she had at least fifty times over the last few days. "I—"

"Love Mike," cut in Isabella. "I know. The whole campus knows. It's like we're all in the middle of a production of *Beauty and the Beast*."

Jessica's cheeks turned pink. "Izzy, come on! Mike loves me, he really does. He—"

"All right, all right." Isabella held up her hands. "Maybe he does love you. And maybe it is none of my business, but I don't want to see you get hurt." She came over to the window, gently putting a hand on Jessica's shoulder. "You are my best friend, you know. I'm really going to miss you."

An unexpected tear came to Jessica's eye. "And I'll miss you," she said truthfully. "It's been great living here."

Isabella leaned closer. "Yeah, but you won't be worrying about me the way I'll be worrying about you."

Jessica brushed the tear from her eye, determined not to let another one escape. "How many times do I have to tell you? There's nothing to worry about. I'm going to be fine."

"Maybe you're right," Isabella said, giving her a hug. "Because at the rate Mike McAllery's moving this morning, you may never move out."

"So, today's the big day, huh?" Danny Wyatt asked as he and Tom Watts left their dorm together and headed across the campus.

Tom looked over at his roommate, a puzzled expression on his face. Tom had been so deep into his own thoughts that he had no idea what Danny was talking about.

Danny gave him a good-natured but amused grin. "The big story, Tom. Remember? The one you and Elizabeth Wakefield have been working on for weeks? *Sports Scandal Rocks Sweet Valley University,*" Danny said in his best newscaster voice. *"Star Players Implicated. Coach Sanchez Says He Was Just Doing His Job."*

"Okay, okay," Tom said, laughing. "Got it. And yes, today's the big day. We run the story this afternoon as a special after the regular news."

It was Tom who had first stumbled onto the story. Some of the biggest athletes on campus were receiving special privileges, including money and academic favors, in return for their "service" to the university. But it was Elizabeth who had done the investigative work on it, even though her ex-boyfriend, Todd Wilkins, had been implicated.

Danny whistled. "Man, I tell you, I wouldn't want to be one of those superjocks for anything when this blows. A few of those guys are going to regret the Christmas they got their first pair of high-tops."

Tom shrugged. "I don't think that much is going to happen right away, to tell you the truth. There'll be a lot of talk and rumor, but it'll take a while for the school to start a real investigation and even longer for them to figure out the truth."

"I'd still like to come by the studio and watch the broadcast, if it's okay," Danny said. He gave his friend a sly, teasing smile. "Unless you and Elizabeth want to be alone, that is."

"Alone with a studio full of camera crew and staff?" Tom asked, equally jokingly. But he refused to look over.

Danny was good at several things—math, wrestling, fixing anything with a plug on the end, making cheesecake—but the thing he had become an expert on lately was knowing when Tom was thinking about Elizabeth Wakefield. It had to be some kind of sixth sense. All Tom had to do was start thinking about Elizabeth, even just in passing, and Danny would immediately bring up her name.

Something had reminded Tom of Elizabeth when they were leaving the dorm, and he'd started wondering again about the poem he'd written for her and left in her mailbox. He'd poured out his heart to her and still hadn't gotten any response that he could make sense of. Had she liked it? Had she even guessed it was from him?

He had thought she would immediately know it

was from him, but things had happened since, like the strange night of the homecoming dance when they'd found each other in the WSVU office. He was upset and angry. He'd thought she'd known he'd written the poem and was mocking him.

So he'd rejected her, told her to go away. And then he'd looked into her eyes and seen so much pain and vulnerability there that he'd known she wasn't laughing at him. That she never would.

It was too late. She'd fled. He'd apologized to her later, and they'd both acted as though nothing had really happened. And things were back to normal—which meant an awkward state of uncertainty. And, for Tom at least, still a little bit of hope.

"Here's where I get off," Danny said as he stopped in front of a large brick building with a terra-cotta roof. "I'll see you and *Elizabeth* later, right? Around four thirty?"

Tom glanced at him sheepishly. He had to admit it wasn't that hard to catch him thinking about Elizabeth. In spite of himself he seemed to be doing it all the time.

"Yeah," Tom agreed, heading toward the journalism building and wondering whether he could bring himself to ask Elizabeth to go for a cup of coffee after the broadcast.

"Tom!" someone called. "I'm so glad I ran into you."

Tom forced Elizabeth out of his mind and turned to find himself looking into the pretty,

7

smiling face of Isabella Ricci. He didn't really know Isabella, but it seemed to him that he often found himself staring into her face lately.

"See, I've got this project to do for sociology on the changing face of Southern California . . ." Isabella said quickly, her words tumbling together, her face flushed. "And I remembered that you did a program last year on the patterns of immigration, and I was wondering if maybe I could see some of your old tapes." She smiled uncertainly. "If it's not too much trouble, I mean. Maybe this afternoon?"

Tom blinked. "This afternoon? Um, I don't know if—"

"See you later," Danny called from the stairs of the brick building. "Four thirty."

"Four thirty," Tom repeated, turning back to Isabella.

"Four thirty," Isabella said, already hurrying away. "That's great."

Tom glanced over at the girl sitting beside him, her blue-green eyes thoughtful, her beautiful face serious and concerned.

He dreamed about being alone with her, he lay awake at night trying to come up with schemes for getting her by herself. And now here she was and he could barely look at her, never mind speak. He'd give anything if he could just reach out and touch her soft cheek with his hand.

Much to his relief, Elizabeth Wakefield had turned up at three thirty to run through the final cut of the sports scandal story with him before the five o'clock screening. She was not only smart and beautiful, she was conscientious as well.

"Well, what do you think?" he managed to ask.

Elizabeth leaned back in her chair and pushed a long strand of golden hair behind her ear. "I think it's excellent," she said slowly. "It's balanced, it's well grounded, it supports its suppositions with facts . . ."

Tom gave his attention to rewinding the tape. "I have a brilliant investigative reporter," he mumbled. "It makes all the difference."

Elizabeth looked over at him, a question in her eyes, but he pretended not to notice.

"So," she said. "Now what, boss?" She sighed. "I feel sort of empty now that this story's over. It was a lot of work, but it was very—"

"Rewarding?" Tom asked, risking eye contact.

Elizabeth smiled, the dimple in her left cheek deepening. Every time she smiled like that he felt as though someone had punched him in the stomach.

"Yes," Elizabeth agreed. "Rewarding. It feels good to do something constructive, to make a difference."

Tom nodded. "I know what you mean. When I think of all the time I wasted playing football . . ." Suddenly he remembered her involvement with Todd Wilkins, the latest star of the SVU basketball team, and tried to backtrack a little. "Not that I don't love football; I love football. I love sports; it's just that—"

There was no way to describe that laugh. It wasn't like silver bells. It wasn't like a mountain spring. It was just the sound of happiness.

"I know what you mean, Tom," Elizabeth assured him. Her gaze fell on the control panel. "I can't tell you what working with you has meant to me. I'm really going to miss—"

"You're quitting?" His gaze had been on the control panel, too, but now it was on her. He knew that he was doing a bad job of trying to keep the look of horror out of his eyes. "You're giving up the station?"

She stared back, baffled. "No, I'm not quitting. I just meant that this story was so important . . . It'll be a long time before another one like that comes along."

Tom was flooded with relief. He cleared his throat. "Not necessarily," he said. The truth was, he had an idea for an exposé that was even more sensational than the sports scandal—but it was also more dangerous. As much as he wanted Elizabeth to work on it with him, he wasn't sure that he could put her at risk.

"What is it, Tom?" She rolled her chair a little closer, her eyes sparkling with excitement. "What is it? You have to tell me."

He pulled his own chair a little closer to her.

10

"It's the fraternity hazings," he said, his voice so low that she had to lean forward to hear. "I was a frat man myself, and I know what goes on behind those doors. Some of it's just stupid fun, but sometimes it gets out of hand." He could see himself in those sea-green eyes. "And I've got this hunch—" He shook his head. "I don't know, that's all it is, Elizabeth, a hunch. But I've got this theory that things are out of hand in at least one of the big fraternities."

"The Sigmas?" Elizabeth asked immediately. She'd already had more than one run-in with Peter Wilbourne III, the arrogant, bigoted president of the Sigmas.

Tom couldn't help himself. His hands were on her shoulders and the words out of his mouth before he knew what he was doing. "That's what I love about you. You always go right to the point."

For one second—or maybe it was only for one hundredth of one second—he thought she was going to grab him back. When she didn't, when he realized how confused and surprised she looked, he dropped his hands as though she'd burnt him.

The door opened behind them. "Here I am," announced a cheerful female voice. "Four thirty, just like you said. Oh, hi, Elizabeth. I didn't know you'd be here."

The look of surprise and confusion on Elizabeth's face changed as her eyes fell on Isabella

11

Ricci, but Tom wasn't sure what it was that it changed to.

"Hi, Isabella." Elizabeth jumped to her feet. "Well, I'd better get going," she said. "I can see you're busy, and I've got a million things to do."

Tom wanted to tell her that she had to stay for the broadcast, but she was hurriedly gathering her books and carefully avoiding his eyes.

"Elizabeth—" he began.

"I'll see you tomorrow," she said, cutting him off. "We can talk about the new assignment then."

"Yeah, sure," he said. "Tomorrow."

Celine Boudreaux, of the Louisiana Boudreaux, gave herself an approving smile in the window of a car as she sauntered across the Sweet Valley University campus. It was a warm and beautiful afternoon, and Celine couldn't help feeling that her contribution to the warmth and beauty of the afternoon wasn't insignificant. She looked drop-dead gorgeous, and she knew it.

But then, I should look pretty gorgeous, she told herself as she pretended not to notice the admiring glances that followed her down the path. *I spent three hours getting ready.*

Not, of course, that anyone would be able to tell how long it had taken her to get that soft, casual, windblown look. Her hair had been pulled and twisted into a mane of curls. Her face had been painstakingly covered and colored. She'd spent twenty minutes alone just making her eyes appear large and round. She smiled to herself. The whole effect was of natural perfection. All in all, it was three hours well spent. A girl couldn't be too careful when she was out for love. Celine wouldn't have cared if it took her ten hours to get herself ready for the man she was after. Once he was hers, it would all be worth it.

Her skirt rustled and her earrings swung as she approached the bench outside the English building. Inside the building, William White was in his last class of the afternoon. Celine knew William's schedule even better than he did. Certainly better than she knew her own schedule.

So far, Celine's attempts to make the proud and mysterious Mr. White fall in love with her had not been too successful. Instead of falling in love with her, he seemed to be falling in love with Celine's roommate, Elizabeth Goody-Two-Shoes Wakefield. But the Boudreaux were not quitters, and Celine was a Boudreaux down to her gold-lacquered toenails. As her granny always said, "The time to stop trying is when you're dead."

There were already two girls sitting on the bench. Celine glanced at them without any curiosity. She would hate to be either of them. Not that they were ugly or even unattractive, but they looked so ordinary. Ordinary and average. Giving them each a small but gracious smile, Celine sat down on the other end of the bench to wait for William.

The girl on her left smiled back. "Hi," she said shyly.

Celine checked her watch. Five more minutes and the advanced course on metaphysical poetry would be getting out.

"I'm in your history class," the girl went on. "My name's Mary."

Celine stifled a groan. She would be named Mary. On the other hand, it had been so long since Celine had attended her history class that it might not be a bad idea to make friends with someone who obviously went to it now and then.

"Oh, of course," Celine drawled. "Mary. You sit . . ."

"At the back," Mary said. She pointed to the other occupier of the bench. "This is Lilly," she announced. "She's in our history class, too."

Lilly smiled.

Celine smiled.

Mary smiled.

Celine glanced at her watch again. Two more minutes. Could she keep smiling like a stuffed toy for two more minutes?

Mary came to her rescue. "You're friends with that gorgeous guy who always dresses in black, aren't you?" she asked suddenly.

Celine blinked. "What?"

"You know," Lilly prompted, suddenly finding her voice. "He's a senior and he has sort of long blond hair and ice blue eyes."

The warm and rewarding feeling of self-satisfaction rushed over Celine. "Yes," she said, slowly and suggestively. "Yes, you could say that we're friends." Her red lips sparkled in the sun. "Close friends."

Lilly and Mary nodded together.

"We've seen you with him," Mary said. "We saw you at the Homecoming dance."

"You are the most beautiful couple," Lilly said.

A sudden, and fairly rare, urge to be friendly overcame Celine. "Do you think so?" she asked. "Do you really think so?"

Lilly and Mary nodded again.

"Oh, yeah. Everybody thinks so."

The doors of the English building suddenly burst open and a crowd of students streamed out, among them the students of the advanced metaphysical poetry class.

"Oh, my gosh," Mary breathed. "There he is."

Celine got to her feet as William White, tall, slender, impossibly handsome, and as arrogant as a young god, slowly descended the steps of the English hall.

"I have to go now," she said to her new friends. "I'll see you around."

"In history," Mary suggested.

Celine nodded vaguely. "Yeah, in history."

She waited until William was almost even with them and then glided up to him, walking so close that it would have been difficult for a passerby to see that they weren't actually arm in arm.

"You'll never guess what those girls I was sitting with said," Celine purred, willing to overlook the fact that he hadn't actually said hello to her.

He gave her the shortest and sharpest of glances. "What girls?"

She nodded behind them. "Those girls back there. Sitting on the bench. They said you and I make an incredibly beautiful couple."

He didn't respond.

"William?" Celine prodded. "They said we make a stunning couple. Everybody thinks so."

There was still no reply. She looked over. He wasn't listening to her; he was watching a girl in a faded pair of jeans and a white T-shirt, her long blond hair casually tied up in the back, as she strode across the lawn.

William wouldn't take his eyes from Elizabeth Wakefield. "Not *everybody* thinks so, Celine," he said.

Elizabeth left WSVU in a state of confusion. *So what's unusual about that?* she asked herself as she hurried out of the building. It seemed as though she was hopelessly jangled and confused every time she left that office. Her encounters with Tom were becoming more and more peculiar. One minute she'd feel such an attraction between them that it was all she could do not to throw herself into his arms, and the next minute they were so far apart one of them might as well have been in

Colorado. It seemed to her that every time she got a little closer to him, she ended up a little farther away.

"Now what?" Elizabeth asked herself. She checked the clock tower at the other end of the quad. It wasn't even five yet, and she didn't really have anywhere to go. She'd thought she was going to watch the broadcast with Tom in the studio, but when Isabella arrived, she realized that he had other plans. It was too early for dinner, and she didn't want to go back to her room yet. Not because Celine, Queen of the Vampires, would still be there. Like the good vampire she was, Celine slept all day and partied all night.

No, the problem with going back to the room was junk food. Elizabeth had been so depressed at the beginning of the semester after the breakup with her longtime boyfriend Todd Wilkins, and the loss of her friendship with Enid—now Alexandra—Rollins, that she'd put on weight. And ever since Celine realized that Elizabeth was on a diet, she'd started leaving opened boxes of cookies and pretzels and bags of chips and candy around the room to tempt her off it.

"Well, speak of the devil," Elizabeth mumbled to herself. Coming toward her were Celine and William White, practically arm in arm. Celine looked smug; William looked bored. Elizabeth pretended not to notice them.

William White was another young man who was

doing his best to confuse her. He seemed to be dating Celine—they certainly spent a lot of time together—but there were other times when Elizabeth was sure that William was flirting with her.

It was just when Elizabeth decided to go to the library and do some work that she noticed a tall young woman, her hair in dozens of tiny braids and a smile on her pretty face, waving to her from the center of the quad.

Nina! Elizabeth smiled back with relief. Nina Harper was a fellow hard worker and dieter, and the only real friend Elizabeth had made since school began. More than that, though, she was sane and funny and as direct as a bullet. Nina always told you exactly what she was thinking. After twenty minutes with Tom Confusion Watts, Nina's sanity, humor, and directness were just what Elizabeth needed. Taking a deep breath, Elizabeth hurried to her friend.

The campus coffeehouse was unusually empty and quiet. So quiet, Elizabeth could hear the little beads on the ends of Nina's braids click together as she shook her head.

"Wow," said Nina, obviously moved. "That's beautiful. It really is beautiful."

Elizabeth looked into her coffee cup. She hadn't planned to tell Nina about the mysterious poem she'd received—she definitely hadn't planned to recite any of it for Nina—but somehow as soon as they sat down she'd found herself blurting it all out.

"That's the most haunting line in the entire poem," Elizabeth explained, "but the rest is just as poignant and well written."

Nina picked up her coffee cup and sighed. "I wish someone would write poems like that to me," she said. "The only person who writes me anything is my grandmother, and those are just notes telling me what she had for dinner or what movie she saw on TV."

"I just wish I knew who wrote it," Elizabeth said. "It's driving me crazy. How could you send someone such an intense and personal poem and not tell them it was from you? What's the point?"

Nina shrugged. "Guys. I'm acing my psychology class, and I can't begin to figure them out." She sipped her drink. "But half a semester of Psych 1 suggests that your mystery poet is probably shy. Or maybe he's been really hurt in the past. You know, he wants to get close to you, but he's afraid."

Elizabeth stared into her cup again. "I was thinking that maybe it's Tom," she said softly. Elizabeth knew in her heart that she *wanted* it to be Tom. For a moment, the night of the Homecoming dance, she'd been sure it wasn't he. But now she was allowing herself to hope again.

"Tom Watts?" Nina laughed. "You think Tom Watts wrote that poem?"

Elizabeth looked up. "You think that's impossible?"

Nina's beads rattled again. "Not impossible, Elizabeth, but unlikely." She made a face. "After all, Tom Watts used to be the biggest jock on this campus. Quarterbacks aren't exactly known for their writing skills, you know. Especially if their nickname was 'Wildman.'"

This wasn't what Elizabeth had wanted to hear. "But Tom's a great writer," she argued. "And he's incredibly intelligent, and original, and—"

Nina's laughter bubbled through the café, as warm and comforting as the aroma of the coffee. "Hang on there!" she cried. "I thought you and Tom were like Batman and Robin. You know, fighting evil and injustice together, but just good friends. It sounds to me like you have a more than professional admiration for the guy."

"It's not that," Elizabeth protested. She could feel herself blushing, but the coffeehouse was so dark that she hoped Nina wouldn't notice. "It's just that I don't think you can assume he can't write poetry because he used to be a football player."

Nina grinned mischievously. "Well, Muhammad Ali wrote poems, so there's a case for the connection between sports and literature, but I really don't think Ali ranks up there with your guy."

Elizabeth, surprised that she had revealed so much of her secret feelings about Tom, retreated. "Oh, you're probably right." The grin vanished. "And anyway, I'm not even sure that Tom is interested in me. He seemed to have some kind of date with Isabella Ricci tonight." She pushed away her cup. "It's just that I can't think of anyone else it could be."

"What about him?" Nina asked.

Him? Nina was gazing over Elizabeth's head at someone. "Him *who*?" Elizabeth whispered back.

"You don't have to turn around," Nina said. "He's coming this way."

A tiny chill ran through Elizabeth as someone brushed against her arm. She looked up to see William White passing their table, Celine close behind.

"He's a poet," Nina said. "And astoundingly beautiful and mysterious."

"And with Celine," Elizabeth pointed out.

Nina raised her cup to her mouth. "He's not with Celine," she said. "Celine's with him."

"I can't believe this," Mike said. "I'm a few minutes late, and you go berserk. You knew I was coming; what's the big deal?"

Mike had finally turned up, nearly two hours late, smiling and talking as though nothing were wrong. It wasn't until they loaded the car and he tried to kiss her that he realized her mood wasn't as good as his.

Jessica kept her eyes on the road ahead of them. "The big deal is that it was not 'a few minutes,' it was one hundred and four," she informed him, trying to keep her voice under control. "And I cut all my morning classes because you said it would be better to move in the morning than at night. But you couldn't miss one little 'business' deal to be on time?"

He took the turn leading off campus a little too sharply.

"That's right," he said. "I couldn't." He looked over at her, but he was wearing sunglasses as black as the finish on a grand piano, so she couldn't see his eyes. "And I'm not used to punching a time clock, baby. Maybe we should get that straight right now. I'm easy to get along with, but don't start expecting me to sign in and out."

Jessica clamped her mouth shut. She was afraid to say anything in case she started to cry. Maybe Isabella was right, maybe she shouldn't move in with Mike. Maybe she was asking for trouble.

Mike reached out and touched her hair. "Don't get all sulky, baby," he scolded her playfully. "You're mad at me now, but you're not going to be mad for long."

She could feel her lower lip tremble. "I'm not mad, Mike," Jessica whispered. "I just don't understand how you could let me down like—"

He pulled away his hand. "That's me," he snapped. "Mike Let-'Em-Down McAllery." He hit the curb pulling into the parking lot of his building. "Ask anybody. Ask my mother, ask my sister, ask your brother . . . I'm completely unreliable.

I've never done an unselfish thing in my life."

"Mike, I didn't mean—" Jessica started to say, but the rest of the sentence died somewhere between her brain and her lips. Mike had pulled into his usual parking space, but right in front of them was something she hadn't expected. It was a beautiful, immaculately perfect dragon's-blood-red Karmann Ghia with a white convertible top. Around the top was a gigantic red bow.

Jessica looked from the car to Mike. He was staring ahead, but she could tell he was waiting for her reaction. There was something in his face that reminded her of a little boy.

"What is that?" she asked in a whisper.

"It's a 1968 Karmann Ghia."

Jessica turned back to the car. She had seen that car before. She'd seen Mike getting into it downtown weeks ago. Only, the car hadn't been beautiful then; the woman driving it had been beautiful, but the car had been a wreck.

"I told you I was trying to buy it for you," Mike said. "I told you I wanted to fix it up for you. Did you think I was kidding? Did you think I was lying?"

She hadn't thought about it at all. She'd been angry seeing him with another woman, but as soon as he'd given her an excuse she'd been so relieved that she'd forgotten about it.

He held up two silver keys. "Come on," he said, "don't you at least want to sit in it?"

Jessica stepped out of the Corvette, tears filling her eyes. "Oh, Mike . . ." she cried. "I never—I'm sorry—I can't believe—"

He stood behind her, his arms around her. "You like it?" he whispered. "I've been working on it day and night, trying to get it ready for when you moved in."

Tears streamed down her cheeks. "Oh, Mike, it's beautiful—"

He turned her around, his breath warm against her skin. "No. You're beautiful. You're the most beautiful thing in my life."

All the anger and frustration of the morning evaporated as Jessica melted into Mike's embrace.

"Don't you two ever do anything besides kiss in public?" asked an angry voice.

Jessica recognized that voice. She pulled away from Mike's lips and turned around.

Steven Wakefield was standing behind them. She'd known she was going to have to face Steven sooner or later—it would be hard to avoid him since he lived in Mike's building—but she hadn't expected it to be this soon.

Mike grinned. "Yeah," he said. "Sometimes we kiss in private, too."

Steven's eyes moved to the boxes stacked in the back of the car. "Don't tell me you're finally moving out," he said. "Don't tell me my prayers have been answered."

"No," Jessica said, "my prayers have been answered." She smiled at her brother as though she didn't know how much he hated Mike McAllery; as though he wasn't telling her every chance he got what bad news Mike was. "I'm moving in."

Steven stared at her as though he didn't quite understand. "You're what?" he asked at last.

"Moving in," Mike said. He smiled. "With me."

"This is going to be the one," Tom Watts was saying in a low whisper. "I feel it in my bones, Elizabeth. This is going to be the biggest story of them all."

He was crouched beside her in the bushes, so close that she only had to breathe deeply to touch him. Elizabeth kept her eyes on the window above them, waiting for a light to go on, waiting for the murmur of conspiring voices to be heard in the room just a wall away.

"I hope so," she whispered back. "I hope you win the Pulitzer for this one, Tom. Nobody deserves it as much as you do. You're the most brilliant investigative reporter there ever was."

"Do you really think so, Elizabeth?" he asked. She could feel him staring at the side of her face in the moonlight. His look was so intense that it was almost as though he were tracing her profile with his hand.

She still refused to turn his way. They were so alone, so close . . . Her heart was spinning out of control. Now was the time to ask him about the poem. Now was the time to say, "Somebody wrote me the most beautiful and moving poem, a poem that could

25

make a woman fall in love. Was it you, Tom?" But she didn't say that. She said, "Of course I do, Tom. Everybody thinks so."

"I don't care about everybody," he answered. "I only care about you." He shifted slightly so that she could now feel his arm, warm against her own. And then he began to recite: "If I dared to love you, if I dared, I might be the keeper of the stars and sky . . ."

She turned while he was speaking. "But coward is my heart, and coward shy," Elizabeth joined in. "I'm too afraid to lose even to try . . ."

He looked into her eyes. "So you did get my poem."

She didn't know whether to laugh or cry. "Tom, why didn't you tell me? Why didn't you tell me it was from you?"

"I was afraid you might laugh at me. I was afraid you might never speak to me again."

She pressed her body against his. "Oh, Tom," she said, her words a sigh. "Oh, Tom—"

Just as her lips touched his there was a sudden flash of light and an explosion. He threw her to the ground, protecting her body with his own. Smoke engulfed them. Elizabeth began to choke. "Tom!" she screamed. "Tom!" But he was gone. She was all alone, in the blinding darkness, in the terrible smoke . . .

Elizabeth opened her eyes, her heart pounding. She'd been dreaming, that's what it was. She'd been dreaming. Dreaming about Tom. Dreaming about the poem . . . She sat up, sniffing the air. She hadn't been dreaming about the smoke. That was real. Frantic that the dorm was on fire, Elizabeth flung herself out of bed.

"Where are you going in your pretty pink pajamas?" asked the unmistakably unpleasant voice of Celine Boudreaux.

Elizabeth froze in the act of jamming her feet into her slippers. She looked up. Celine was sitting at her desk, holding a sheet of notebook paper in one hand and a cigarette in the other. Elizabeth recognized the paper immediately. It was the poem. Celine was reading her poem!

Celine held up the piece of paper and waved it in the air. "What's this?" she asked with a leer. "Is this the poem from Little Miss America's secret admirer?"

Elizabeth sat back down, kicking off her slippers. "Put it away, Celine," she ordered. "If you don't, I'm going to make sure your English professor finds out that that paper you wrote for your midterm exam was written five years ago by a Sigma."

Celine made a face. "Oooh," she said in a little-girl voice. "Who woke up on the wrong side of bed?"

"I mean it," Elizabeth said, getting back under the covers. "I know for a fact that you paid twenty-five dollars for that paper." She smiled sweetly. "I think your teacher would be interested in finding out about that, don't you?"

Celine stubbed out her cigarette. "I wouldn't try blackmailing me, Princess Pill," she growled.

"I don't like you as it is. You wouldn't want to make me mad." But she put the poem back on Elizabeth's desk and got into her own bed.

Elizabeth turned her face to the wall. "I don't want to make you mad, Celine," she said quietly. "I just want to make you disappear."

Chapter Two

"Go away, Anoushka," Winston Egbert pleaded. "Please. If they catch me talking to you, I'll have *two* bricks around my neck tomorrow."

Anoushka didn't go away. Instead, she stepped in front of him, blocking his path. "Are you stupid or something, Winnie?" she demanded. "Why are you letting them treat you like this? Can't you see it's demeaning?"

Winston sighed, partly in exasperation, and partly because he'd been wearing a brick around his neck for two days now and his neck was killing him.

"It's not demeaning, Anoushka," Winston insisted. "It's part of the male fraternal ritual, that's all." He gave her what he hoped was a pitying and not a pained look. "Not that I'd expect you to understand."

Anoushka made a face. "Why not?" she asked. "Because I'm too intelligent?"

He would have shaken his head, but he'd learned the hard way that it was incredibly difficult to shake your head when you had a brick around your neck. "No," Winston answered, stepping around her and starting to walk again, "because you're a woman. Women don't understand these things."

"Oh, really?" Anoushka said. "And just what is it that we don't understand?"

Winston looked uneasily around. They were still far enough from the main campus that it was unlikely a Sigma spy would spot him talking to Anoushka, but you couldn't be too careful. He was wearing the brick in the first place because he'd forgotten to call a Sigma brother "sir."

"Well?" Anoushka pushed. "What is it we don't understand?"

"First of all, you don't understand that hazing is good, clean fun," Winston explained patiently. "Second, you don't understand that no one ever gets hurt. This is just a male bonding ritual, Anoushka, not some form of torture."

"Oh, sure," Anoushka said, her eyes on the brick banging against his chest as he moved. "That's what it looks like, Win. A male bonding ritual. Maybe if there was some blood, I would have recognized it right away."

He trudged on. "And the other thing you don't understand is that *nobody* depledges a fraternity just because he doesn't want to wear a brick around his neck."

She eyed him coolly. "No? And why is that, Winnie? Maybe you can explain it to me in simple terms."

"Of course I can," Winston said. "It's because no one wants all the other guys to think he's a complete loser."

Elizabeth arrived at her first class of the day with a new sense of determination and energy. It had felt good giving Celine back as good as she gave last night. It had even felt good being blown up in her dream.

Once Elizabeth had really thought about the dream, she'd understood that it wasn't about her feelings for Tom. It was about never being distracted from your work by something as transitory as romance. In the dream, if she had concentrated on the job at hand instead of getting sappy about Tom and the poem, the dream wouldn't have ended with them being bombed, it would have ended with them winning the Pulitzer Prize. From now on, Elizabeth wasn't going to moon around, wondering who wrote the poem. She wasn't going to let Celine drive her crazy. No, she was going to throw herself into her new assignment with Tom as she had never thrown herself into an assignment before.

Elizabeth stopped at the top of the stairs leading down to the humanities complex. Right in front of her, hobbling along with a brick tied around his neck on a thick cord, was just the person she needed to help her throw herself into her new assignment.

"Winston!" Elizabeth shouted.

She was sure he must have heard her, but he didn't slow down or even look up. She hoisted her backpack over her shoulder and hurried after him.

"Hey, wait for me!" she called, coming up beside him. "I need to talk to you."

"Not now," Winston answered without even moving his lips. "Later. Call me tonight or something."

Elizabeth laughed. "I'm not going to call you tonight," she said. "Come on, Win, I want to talk to you now."

"Shhh," he hissed. "Don't make so much noise. You'll draw attention to us."

Elizabeth gave him a bewildered look. "You mean more attention than you walking around with a brick?"

"Elizabeth, I mean it!" There was real terror in his voice. "Go away. I'm not supposed to talk to anyone without a Sigma's permission. You're going to get me in trouble."

"But that's exactly what I want to talk to you about," Elizabeth said. "About hazing. Tom and I are going to do an exposé—"

Winston made the sound of something losing a lot of air very quickly. At last he looked at her, but his eyes were practically popping with panic. "Geez, are you kidding me? You want me to be ceremonially hanged in the quad or something? I can't help you with an article on hazing. I—"

Everything in Winston Egbert stopped at once. His mouth stopped moving, his eyes stopped focusing, he ceased breathing.

"What is it?" Elizabeth asked, glancing over her shoulder. It was Peter Wilbourne III, president of the Sigmas, bigot, bully, and general creep. Elizabeth had reasons of her own for avoiding Peter Wilbourne. The first was that ever since the Theta-Sigma party where she told him what she thought of him, Peter Wilbourne had done everything he could to frighten and torment her. The second reason was that Peter Wilbourne was under the mistaken impression that he and Elizabeth had gone to the Homecoming game together and shared a public kiss. In fact it had been Jessica pretending to be Elizabeth on a dare from her sorority, Theta Alpha Theta.

"Did I see your lips moving?" Peter Wilbourne shouted. "I don't remember giving you permission to speak."

"I'll see you later, Win," Elizabeth whispered, hurrying past him. But as soon as she was a few yards away she looked back.

"Get down on the ground and give me fifty, Sigma plebe!" Peter barked.

"Yes, sir!" Winston snapped back, falling to the ground, brick and all.

"I can't believe it," Elizabeth mumbled to herself. "How can he let that moron treat him like that?"

"Do you want to know what he told me?"

Elizabeth turned around to find Anoushka, one of the girls from Winston's dorm, standing beside her.

"I'd love to hear it," Elizabeth said.

"He doesn't want the other guys to think he's a loser."

"Mr. Esposito doesn't know what he's talking about," Nina Harper said to herself as she strode across the campus on the way back from a meeting with her adviser. "I'm getting everything out of college that I should be getting. I'm well rounded."

Clusters of students were standing in groups or sitting on the grass, just talking and hanging out, but Nina passed them all without a wave. She didn't know how other people found so much time to socialize. As far as Nina was concerned, college wasn't about sports, or clubs, or parties.

"I didn't come here to play chess or watch football games," she'd told Mr. Esposito. "I came here to get an education." Mr. Esposito told her he didn't think that the classroom was the only place to get an education. He thought she should take an interest in other things. "I don't have time to take an interest in other things," Nina had informed him. "I'm too busy working."

Nina sighed to herself as she climbed the library stairs. Deep in her heart, she knew there was some truth in what Mr. Esposito had said. Even she was getting a little tired of doing nothing but going to classes, studying, sleeping, and going to more classes. If it weren't for Elizabeth Wakefield, she wouldn't even have one friend to talk to and have the occasional cup of coffee with.

She came to a stop in the library foyer, thinking about Elizabeth. Elizabeth studied almost as hard as Nina did, and had her journalism as well. Nina had noticed the change in Elizabeth since she began working with Tom Watts at WSVU, the campus television station. She was happier than she'd been during the first weeks of school, and full of enthusiasm and excitement. Not only that, Elizabeth's academic work hadn't suffered because she was running around acting like Lois Lane. If anything, it had improved. Elizabeth had more energy for everything now.

"What do you think?" asked a deep voice behind her. "Are you going to go?"

Nina turned around, startled. Standing very close to her was Bryan Nelson.

There were three reasons Nina knew who Bryan Nelson was. He was the only other black student in her advanced chemistry class, he was the only guy on campus who wore his hair in almost the same way she wore hers, and he was one of the best-looking men in the entire university.

Bryan was smiling at her. "Well?" he asked. "Are you going?"

Even if she knew what he was talking about—which she didn't—she probably wouldn't have been able to answer. She wasn't sure if it was his incredible smile, like the sun coming up on a perfect day, or his pale hazel eyes, but there was something about Bryan Nelson that chased everything else out of her mind.

He pointed to the bulletin board they were standing in front of. "The Black Students Union meeting," he said. "It could be interesting."

Nina looked at the notice. The Black Students Union was holding a special colloquium on African-Americans making it in a white-dominated business world. Mr. Esposito would definitely want her to go. Not only did he think she needed some extracurricular activity, he thought she should take more interest in ethnic issues.

"Oh, I don't think so," she answered, turning back to Bryan. "I don't really have time. I have a big physics test the next day."

Bryan made a disappointed face. "That's too bad. I was hoping we could go for a pizza or something afterward." He gave her another five-hundred-megawatt smile. "Maybe next time."

"Yeah," agreed Nina, feeling a little disappointed herself. "Maybe next time."

"It's like my granny always says," Celine informed her reflection.

Instead of the elaborate dresses and flowing

skirts she usually wore, Celine was wearing a simple, low-cut Lycra top and stretch pants. "There's more than one way to skin a polecat." She gave herself a sly smile. "And more than six ways to cook him."

William White seemed to go for the Elizabeth Wakefield casual look, so the casual look was what he was getting tonight. She daubed a little more perfume between her breasts. Casual but sexy. She fastened a small gold heart around her neck. Sexy but sincere.

There was a knock at the door. Celine instantly threw herself onto her bed and picked up the book that was lying there. She stretched into a relaxed, casual position. "Come in," she called. "The door's open."

William stepped into the room. His eyes went to Elizabeth's side of the room first, then slowly moved over to Celine's.

"She's not here," Celine said, a little more sharply than she'd intended. "She's out grocery shopping."

William let his cool blue eyes rest on her. There was no sign in them that he had heard what she said, or that it meant anything to him. That was one of the things Celine admired most about William White: he never really showed his hand.

"So what is it you wanted to see me about, Celine?" he asked. "What was so urgent it couldn't wait until tomorrow?"

She patted the space beside her on the bed. "Come over here," she coaxed. "I have something to show you."

He smiled one of his slow, self-satisfied smiles, his eyes on the cleavage showing above her skimpy top. "I think you're already showing it, Celine," he commented. "I really don't need to see any more."

Celine gave him a self-satisfied smile of her own. "Don't be stupid," she said sweetly. "This is something you do need to see." She slid her hand under her pillow and pulled out a sheet of lined notebook paper.

In spite of himself, he was curious. She could see a tiny flicker of interest in those frozen eyes. "What is it?"

Celine leaned back on the pillow, slowly unfolding the piece of paper. "It's a poem," she said simply.

"A poem?" One pale eyebrow rose quizzically. "You're writing poems now, Celine? That doesn't sound like you. Poison pen letters, maybe, but not poems."

She allowed a smile to cross her lips. "Oh, I didn't write it." She raised her eyes to his. "It's a love poem. To Elizabeth."

He was beside her so fast, she barely saw him move. "Who wrote it?" he asked, taking it from her hand as he sat down on the bed.

She watched his face while he read the poem. "I don't know who wrote it," she said softly. "I don't think the Little Princess knows herself."

He looked up, the interest more than a flicker now. "Really? Are you sure?"

"Pretty sure," Celine said. "Of course," she said, looking at him under half-closed lids, "I could be surer. I could probably even find out who did write it."

Another thing she liked about William was that he didn't waste time.

"How could you find out?" he asked.

She twisted a strand of her honey-colored hair around one finger. "Well, the way I figure it, there are only two people it's likely to be."

"Tom Watts," William said in almost a whisper. Celine nodded. "Tom Watts."

"And the second person?" William prompted.

"Peter Wilbourne," Celine purred. She caught the protest in his eyes. "I know they had that horrible scene at the Theta-Sigma party," Celine said quickly. "But that was a long time ago. Long before he kissed her at the Homecoming game."

William leaned back against the pillow, too, his eyes on the ceiling, deep in thought.

"Find out," he said at last.

"I'll do better than that," Celine said. "I'll not only find out, I'll help keep them apart."

He looked over at her. "Why are you doing this? Why are you helping me?"

Celine shrugged. "I'm bored," she said. "I need a little fun."

After William had gone, Celine sat on the bed, smiling like a cat that had just wiped out the entire bird population of Southern California. William White might think he was cool and invulnerable, but Celine knew better. Elizabeth Wakefield was his weakness. Celine saw it as the attraction of evil to good. William was interested in Elizabeth because she was so perfect and innocent. He wanted to corrupt her. He wanted to control her. And when he'd gotten what he wanted, he'd dump Elizabeth quicker than a squirrel drops an empty shell.

That was why Celine had decided to change her tactics. Instead of trying to turn William against Elizabeth, she was going to help him win her. Then, after he destroyed Elizabeth and turned to Celine, his confidante, his co-conspirator, the person who had gotten him what he wanted, Celine was going to destroy him.

It was like Celine's granny always said: *She who laughs last, laughs best.*

Jessica was getting ready for the first sorority event since she'd been pledged to Theta Alpha Theta, the most prestigious house on campus. She wasn't thinking about the Thetas, though, or what the social would be like. She was thinking about Mike McAllery. And love.

Jessica smiled as she looked around the bathroom. Mike's terry-cloth robe was hanging from the back of the door; his shaving equipment was on the sink. His socks were in a little pile in the corner. She lay back in the tub with a contented sigh.

"If my friends could see me now," she told the jasmine-scented bubbles. "They'd die, that's what they'd do. They'd just die." Even Lila Fowler, the newly married Countess di Mondicci, would die if she could see Jessica now, living with a man in a gorgeous apartment.

An unpleasant thought entered Jessica's mind. If her parents could see her now, they might die, too. And they'd probably kill her before they did. Jessica escorted the thought back out of her head. She didn't want to think of anything unpleasant right now. She was too happy.

She sank into the bubbles. Until a few days ago, Jessica had thought that she knew what it was to be happy. She'd thought she'd been happy a lot of the time. Shopping made her happy. Parties made her happy. Just hanging out with her friends in the Dairi Burger back in Sweet Valley used to make her happy. But since she moved in with Mike, Jessica had come to understand that those feelings of happiness were nothing. It was like someone in Alaska thinking she knew what summer was and then moving to Florida.

"Why didn't anybody tell me that living with a man would be like this?" Jessica asked her washcloth. "It's the most wonderful thing in the world."

She couldn't decide which part she liked best. She loved coming home from a late class or meeting, knowing he'd be waiting for her. She loved getting home first and listening for his footsteps in the hall. She loved cooking with him, and eating with him, and even washing the dishes together. She loved just sitting in front of the television, curled up together, watching what was on the screen, between their kisses. She loved waking up in the morning with his arm across her and his mouth against her hair.

"No wonder so many people write love songs," Jessica said as she got out of the tub. "It's the best thing there is."

The only trouble was, Jessica really couldn't talk to anyone about her happiness. Isabella was her best friend, but she didn't want to hear about Mike. Isabella was sure he was going to break Jessica's heart. And as far as everyone else was concerned, Jessica was still living in the dorm.

Even Elizabeth didn't know the truth. Somehow Jessica sensed that as angry as Steven was, he wasn't going to tell their parents what was going on. He wasn't going to break one important, long-standing, and unspoken agreement: you don't tell on your siblings. Elizabeth, she wasn't so sure about.

And not only was Jessica worried about her parents finding out, she was afraid the Thetas might drop her if they discovered she had moved

42

in with Mike. Her sorority sisters didn't like Mike McAllery any more than Steven Wakefield did.

She was in the bedroom, putting the finishing touches on her makeup when the front door opened.

"Where's my baby?" Jessica heard the most wonderful voice in the world call.

Jessica tossed down her lipstick, rushed out of the room, and threw herself into his arms.

"What are you all dressed up for?" he asked, holding her close for a kiss. "I thought we were doing the shopping tonight. Isn't that what boring old couples do on a Thursday night?"

Reluctantly, Jessica pulled away from his lips. "Not this Thursday, they don't," she told him. "This Thursday one of them stays home and finishes the pasta from last night and the other goes to a social at the Theta house."

Mike groaned. "You can't be serious." He rested his chin on the top of her head. "I've been thinking about coming home to you all day long. This is the one place I want to be."

Jessica hugged him tightly. "I don't want to go, Mike, but I have to. If I don't show up for the first social, they'll want to know why."

He moved away a few inches, looking her in the eye. "So tell them. Tell them you just moved in with me and we want some time to ourselves. What's the problem with that?"

"You know what they're like," she said evasively.

43

Now didn't seem like the right time to explain their attitude toward him; that if the Thetas had had their way, Jessica would have given Mike up long ago.

"They think they're more important than anything else," she finished lamely.

"And what about you?" he asked, kissing her forehead. "Do you think they're more important than anything else?"

"Mike!" She hugged him hard. "How can you ask that? You know you're the most important thing in my life."

His lips moved to hers. "Then why are you spending the evening with the Thetas?" he asked.

Jessica tried to answer. But it got lost in their kiss.

Elizabeth's face was flushed with excitement as she marched down the hall of WSVU to Tom's office. Since yesterday's broadcast of the sports scandal story, the campus had been talking about little else.

She was still hurt that Tom hadn't asked her to watch it with him yesterday, but she was feeling so pleased with the job they'd done that it didn't seem right not to share this feeling with him.

Elizabeth opened the door of Tom's office without knocking. He was sitting at his desk, absorbed in something he was writing.

"We did it!" Elizabeth said as she came through the door. "We really did it! I think over half the

44

campus must have seen your broadcast, and the other half heard about it. People have been coming up to me all day long, congratulating me."

At the sound of her voice, Tom turned around. "They've been coming up to me all day, too," he said, getting to his feet, "but it hasn't always been to congratulate me." He smiled happily. "We've done it this time, Elizabeth. I feel like a wanted man. Every jock I pass makes some rude gesture or mumbles some threat." He reached out and grabbed her hands.

She squeezed back, laughing. "You're the only person I know who would think it was fun to be in trouble with some of the most important guys on campus."

He swung her around. "But this is what it's about. Really doing something. Really making people look around and take notice." He stopped spinning, but didn't let go of her hands. "It's great, Elizabeth. It's absolutely, incredibly great—and most of it's thanks to you. You are the most brilliant investigative reporter I've ever worked with. Promise me you'll never leave."

"I promise," Elizabeth said, still laughing. "I'll never leave WSVU."

He continued to look at her for a few seconds, his expression serious. Then, abruptly, he let go of her and went back to his desk. "Dean Shreeve wants to see us tomorrow morning," he said over his shoulder. "With your notes."

"Dean Shreeve?" Elizabeth had seen Dean Shreeve, the dean of students, at the orientation ceremony the first day of school, but not since. "Is this good news or bad news?"

"Good news," Tom said, still with his back to her. "The school's going to set up an official investigation. And one of the big L.A. papers is sending a reporter down to talk to you and me about our story."

"That's amazing!" Elizabeth exclaimed. "That's even better than we'd hoped."

He looked over his shoulder at her and smiled. "We can't rest on our laurels, though. We have to roll right on with the hazing story." He turned his chair to face her again. "What about Winston? Did you get to talk to him?"

Winston! She'd been so excited about the reaction to the sports story that she'd forgotten about Winston. He was probably still doing push-ups in the quad.

"Poor Win," she said. "You should have seen him this morning, Tom. He was trudging around campus with a brick around his neck."

Tom shook his head. "That's usually the first stage of plebe humiliation. Sounds like your friend Peter Wilbourne must have it in for Winston." A dark look flashed in his eyes. "Man, would I like to nail that guy," he mumbled, half to himself. "That is one guy I'd really like to see get what he deserves."

"Me too," Elizabeth said. "And we're probably just the people to make sure he does."

Steven Wakefield was about to take his wallet out to pay for the groceries when something caught his attention at the other end of the store.

"Steven," said his girlfriend, Billie, giving him a nudge. "The woman's waiting."

Steven kept staring at the entrance. "Did you see that?" he asked.

Billie followed his eyes. "I don't know what you're talking about," she said. "The display of cookies? The special on avocados?"

"Twenty-three dollars and fifteen cents," the cashier repeated.

Steven looked over at Billie. "You really didn't see them?"

Billie groaned. "Them? What *them* are we talking about? Not Jessica Wakefield and Mike McAllery, by any chance?"

The cashier cleared her throat. "Excuse me, sir," she said, "but if you could just give me the twenty-three dollars and fifteen cents . . . There are a few people waiting behind you."

Steven snapped his fingers. "Aha! So you did see them. I knew you couldn't have missed them."

"Hey, buddy!" the man behind them shouted. "Do you think you could pay and continue this conversation in your car?"

"Steven," Billie said between clenched teeth.

"I did not see them. And I don't want to see them. I just want you to pay for our food so we can go."

Steven couldn't understand it. Ordinarily, he and Billie saw eye to eye on most things. Of all the people he knew, she was one of the most intelligent, levelheaded, and clear thinking. But ever since Jessica started seeing Mike McAllery, he'd been seeing a side of Billie he'd never seen before. The flaky, illogical, incautious side. The side that didn't see anything wrong with *his* little sister going out with a man who was not only older, but the owner of a fast car, a fast motorcycle, and a bad reputation.

"Billie," Steven said, trying to be calm and reasonable. "Jessica and Mike are in here shopping."

She gazed at him in wonder. "Steven," she said, "this is a supermarket. That's why people come here. To buy food."

"Except that most of them would like to take their food home," the man behind them said.

"That doesn't upset you?" Steven asked. "My sister is grocery shopping with this man she's *living* with, and that doesn't upset you?"

"If you don't give me the twenty-three dollars and fifteen cents," the cashier said, "I'm going to have to call the manager."

"Steven," Billie said, "*I'm* in here grocery shopping with the man I'm living with. Should I be upset about that, too?"

Steven removed twenty-five dollars from his wallet and handed it to the cashier. "That's typical of you, Billie, isn't it?" he asked as he waited for his change. "If you don't want to discuss something, you change the subject."

Chapter Three

"So the first thing I do when I get into this gorgeous car is back it into his bike. Can you believe it?" Jessica asked Isabella, laughing.

The two of them were eating lunch in the café, and Jessica had told Isabella in full detail about the Karmann Ghia Mike had fixed up for her.

"You should've seen his face! He's been working on that bike for years." Jessica smiled at the tabletop, remembering Mike's face. "But he wasn't even mad. He just said he'd make sure not to park behind me anymore."

Isabella lifted the top of her hamburger bun. "What a sport."

Jessica beamed at her friend. She was so glad to see Isabella. The only person she seemed to talk to anymore was Mike, and as wonderful as that was, it was nice to talk to a girl for a change. "I'm so happy I ran into you," Jessica said, helping herself to one of Isabella's fries. "It seems like ages since I've seen you."

Isabella smiled. It was a thin, ironic smile. "It has been ages, Jess. The only time I see you anymore is when you're rushing to a class or rushing away from one."

Jessica stirred the ice in her glass with her straw. She didn't really want to talk about how little she'd seen of Isabella since she moved out of the dorm; she wanted to talk about Mike. "Well, you know how it is," she said with a rueful shrug. "I guess that's the disadvantage of living off-campus. Plus, there's so much to do in the apartment. And there's shopping, and cleaning . . ." Jessica smiled meaningfully. "And, you know, just hanging out . . ."

Isabella opened a packet of ketchup and squeezed it on her hamburger. "Sounds like fun."

Jessica decided to ignore the trace of sarcasm in Isabella's voice. "It is fun, Izz," she said enthusiastically. "It really is." The dimple appeared in her left cheek as she smiled. "Did I tell you what happened the other night? When Mike and I went shopping? He went to get the cereal while I went to get some cheese." She laughed at the memory. "He was gone for hours. I got the cheese, and the yogurt, and some canned tomatoes, and he still hadn't come back."

"There's nothing strange about that," Isabella muttered only half under her breath. "He probably went out for a beer."

Jessica decided to ignore this, too. "So finally I went looking for him, and do you know where he was?"

Isabella shook her head. "No, Jess. Where was he?"

"He was still in the cereal aisle! It was so funny. He must've looked at every kind they had. He couldn't make up his mind whether he wanted the one with the free miniature flashlight inside or the one with the minitransformer." She wiped a tear of laughter from her eye. "Guys are too funny, aren't they?"

"Um, yeah." Isabella chewed thoughtfully on her hamburger. "So when was this shopping expedition?" she asked at last. "It wasn't the night of the Theta social, by any chance?"

"The Theta social?" Jessica raised her glass to her lips. "Of course it wasn't," she lied. "I told you, I had really bad cramps that night. I couldn't move from the couch."

"Sure," Isabella said. She picked a stray sliver of onion from the tabletop. "It's just that it seems so unlike you, missing an important event like that. You used to be the girl who wouldn't miss a party if she were in traction."

"I still am," Jessica said firmly. "I don't know why you're getting on my case like this. You know belonging to the Thetas is one of the most important things in the world to me. But I was really in pain. I felt like I was going to die."

Isabella arched one eyebrow. "Alison Quinn thought that maybe you *had* died, Jess. She couldn't believe you missed the first pledge social." She licked some ketchup from her fingers. "Nobody could."

Jessica groaned inwardly. So that was what this was all about. Alison Quinn, the snooty vice president of Theta Alpha Theta, must have said something to Isabella about Jessica's absence. "Well, you can tell Alison I'll be at the next event for sure," she said.

"You'd better be," Isabella said, not unkindly. She reached out and touched Jessica's hand. "I know you're all wrapped up in Mike right now, but you've got to remember that there are other things in your life, too, Jess. And there won't be if you're not careful. You know what the Thetas are like. Alison and Magda are unhappy enough about your sister. They won't think twice about dumping you."

Jessica stared blankly at her friend. "My sister?" Somehow, she had completely forgotten about her sister. Relations between the twins hadn't been particularly good since they started college, but since she'd moved off-campus, Jessica hadn't thought about Elizabeth very much at all. Thinking about Elizabeth meant feeling guilty— for having moved out of the room they shared the first week of school, for not having told her about moving in with Mike. And guilt was Jessica's least

54

favorite emotion. "What about my sister?"

"You don't know?" Isabella wiped her mouth with a paper napkin. "Elizabeth withdrew her pledge from the Thetas. She said she's too busy working for WSVU to put time into a sorority, but I have the feeling Alison's suspicious about that date with Peter Wilbourne. I think she's pretty much figured out that it wasn't Elizabeth who kissed Peter at the Homecoming game, but you."

"Even my own sister's against me," Jessica said, groaning out loud. "Why doesn't anybody want me to be happy?" She sighed and stared out the window. "I'm so glad I have Mike. At least he really cares about me."

Isabella noisily drained the last drops of soda from her cup and gave Jessica a look. "I knew we couldn't spend more than thirty seconds talking about something besides Mike."

Winston lay facedown on his bed, the heating pad he'd borrowed from one of his dormmates over the back of his neck.

"This is worth it," Winston told himself as the warmth of the pad gradually spread across his shoulders. "No pain, no gain."

"You know, it is possible to have pain without any gain at all," said a voice in the doorway.

If it had been any other voice, the agony Winston was feeling after another day of wearing a brick necklace would have stopped him from turning to the door. But this was the voice of Denise Waters. In Winston Egbert's world, Denise Waters was the nicest, most intelligent, and most beautiful woman alive.

Slowly, trying not to wince or groan out loud, Winston looked toward the door. It was worth it. Denise Waters's lovely face was suffused with sympathy.

"Oh, Winnie," she cried, coming over to the bed. "Look at you. You don't look like you're joining a fraternity, you look like you're being murdered."

He stopped himself from saying that he was beginning to feel like it, too.

"This is just temporary," Winston answered, hoping he sounded tough and manly. "It's sort of like having your legs waxed or something. You know, it hurts like hell while it's happening, but it's worth it in the end."

Winston had been living in Oakley Hall, an all-female dorm except for him, for almost two months now, and he knew a lot more than he used to about things like leg waxing.

"It's nothing like having your legs waxed," Denise said flatly. She sat on the floor beside him. "Leg waxing has a purpose. The only purpose of this is to make your Sigma buddies feel like big men because they can push you around."

"You don't understand," Winston protested. There had been several times over the last few days of hazing when he wasn't sure that he understood himself. Times when he found himself publicly groveling at the feet of Peter Wilbourne or one of his cronies, or having to bite back a shout of pain and pretend he didn't mind being physically tortured.

But he wanted to be a Sigma more than anything. In high school he'd been Winston, the joke. In college he wanted to be Winston, the big man on campus. He wanted to walk around in that blue jacket with the other Sigmas, joking around with each other, envied by the poor losers who didn't have what it took to make the grade. "This is the way I prove my loyalty."

Denise gave him a look as she readjusted the pad. "That better?"

"A little more to the left, maybe," Winston said. Her hand brushed his back as she moved the heating pad a little to the left.

Winston's solar plexus began to dissolve. Maybe this torture really was worth it. He'd walk over hot coals if it meant having Denise Waters touch his skin.

"Can I get you anything else?" Denise asked. "You want some soup or a cold drink or something?"

Winston shook his head, very slightly. Horrible things happened to his neck muscles when he moved his head too suddenly. "No, it's all right. I have to go soon anyway."

"Go?" Denise eyed him sharply. "Go where?"

"Over to Sigma house," Winston answered.

"You're going to Sigma house?" She sounded incredulous. "Winston, you can barely walk. What's wrong with you?"

"Nothing's wrong with me." He flashed her one of his biggest and brightest smiles. "Duty calls."

"Duty's not the only one calling."

Winston and Denise both looked over. Anoushka was at the door. "Elizabeth Wakefield's on the phone, Winnie. She wants to talk to you."

That's all I need, Winston thought miserably. *Elizabeth on my case, too.*

He struggled to sit up without grunting or groaning. "Tell her I'm not here. Please?" he begged.

"Yeah," Denise said, slapping the pad down on him so hard he yelped. "Tell her he's out being a big man on campus."

"It just seems really odd to me, that's all," Celine said. She batted her eyes, drying the mascara she'd just applied. "Back home, a woman always knows who her admirers are."

Elizabeth's head was bent over her desk and she didn't look up. "Leave me alone, will you, Celine? You should never have read my private stuff in the first place." She scratched out something she'd written with heavy lines. "And even if I did know who sent me that poem, you'd be the last person I'd tell."

58

Celine leaned against her dresser, striking a pose. "Now, let's see . . ." She pretended to be thinking hard. "There aren't that many men it could be, are there? There's Peter Wilbourne, of course. You and he did exchange a pretty impressive kiss at the Homecoming game . . ."

Elizabeth's eyes flashed. "You know that wasn't me," she said. "You know I was here by myself the day of the Homecoming game. Jessica was the one who made a public spectacle of herself with that creep."

Celine slowly twisted a strand of hair around her finger. "Of course I know," she said. "But Peter doesn't, does he? He still believes it was you." She drew her eyebrows together, still thinking hard. "But you're right, it's unlikely to be him." A sly smile came to her deep red lips. "And then of course there's my own sweet William . . ."

Elizabeth didn't look up at this, but her cheeks flushed.

"Or Tom Watts," Celine threw out casually. "You spend a lot of time with him, don't you? Maybe he's your little poet."

Elizabeth flinched.

The sly smile settled on Celine's lips. Elizabeth might not know who wrote that slushy, gushy poem, but she probably knew who she'd like it to be. Not Peter Wilbourne III, that was for sure. And probably not William White the One and Only, either.

"Don't be ridiculous," Elizabeth mumbled, still not looking at her. "Tom and I have a working relationship, and that's all."

Celine pulled a hooded white mohair sweater over her head. Mohair wasn't something every girl could get away with, but Celine knew that she could. Against her honey-colored curls and pale complexion, the effect was almost angelic.

"I guess it isn't very important anyway," Celine said, her eyes on Elizabeth's reflection in the mirror. "I mean, one itsy-bitsy poem isn't much to get excited about, is it?" She picked up her bag and slung it over her shoulder.

Elizabeth snapped off the tip of her pencil, but said nothing.

"See ya later, sugar," Celine drawled, seeping out of the room. "Don't wait up for me. There's a party at the Sigmas, so I'll be home late."

Elizabeth didn't say good-bye.

Celine was in a good mood as she struck out from Dickenson Hall. It was early evening, but though the campus was quiet, there were still lots of students on the lawns and paths of the main quad, and lights on in almost every building.

"Tom Watts," Celine whispered to herself as she walked down a lighted path. "The mystery poet has to be Tom Watts."

She'd led William to believe that Peter might be a possibility because she wanted to lay her trap for William as wide as possible, but in her own mind there wasn't any doubt. Ever since Elizabeth started working at WSVU with Tom, she'd begun to change. She was becoming stronger, sharper, and feistier. Instead of letting Celine badger and depress her, she either fought back or treated Celine like a bug—irritating but insignificant.

Besides that, Elizabeth was looking better. She was still a little heavier than she'd been at the beginning of school, but even Celine couldn't deny that her roommate was attractive. And lately she'd been developing a distinctive style of her own. It wasn't a style that appealed to Celine, of course, but it obviously appealed to others. Tom Watts, for instance. Celine scowled. And William White.

She came to a stop at the entrance to the television studio. *Why not?* she asked herself. From what she knew of Tom Watts, the chances were that he'd be in there, beavering away to bring truth and justice to Sweet Valley U. If she was right, and she was sure she was right—Celine hadn't inherited the Boudreaux women's highly developed sense of intuition for nothing—then the sooner she started meddling in his relationship with Elizabeth, the sooner William White would be hers.

Celine pulled her pocket mirror from her bag, checked that her makeup hadn't smudged or her hair gone limp in her walk from the dorm, pushed open the studio door, and walked straight into Tom Watts.

He started to walk around her, but she held him with one pale, slender hand. "Tom Watts!" she exclaimed, her voice warm as a kitten and sweet as syrup. "You don't know me, but I've heard all about you."

Tom glanced at her hand as though there were claws at the end of it rather than long, sparkling red nails.

"I'm Celine. Celine Boudreaux," she continued in a rush. "Elizabeth Wakefield's roommate."

At the mention of Elizabeth's name his whole demeanor changed. Instead of quiet and wary hostility, his face softened into a smile.

My God, Celine thought. *This man is gorgeous.* Too intense and serious and bound up with principles for her taste, of course, but gorgeous all the same.

What was it about Elizabeth Wakefield that attracted these extraordinary men? Celine was beginning to feel like the Wicked Queen in *Snow White.* Every time she looked in the magic mirror and asked who was the most beautiful of all, the answer wasn't *you* anymore.

He held out his hand. "Elizabeth's roommate," he said politely. "Glad to meet you."

"Not as glad as I am to meet you," Celine purred. "I just had to stop by and tell you what a great job you and Elizabeth did on that sports story. I saw the broadcast, and I thought it was just fantastic."

"Elizabeth deserves the credit," Tom said

quickly. "She did all the investigative work."

"You're too modest," Celine chided. "Elizabeth told me how hard you worked . . . and how much you put into it. She said she finds you an inspiration."

Tom flushed. "Really?"

"She has a very high opinion of you," Celine said. "But you must know that." Her smile was an invitation.

An invitation that Tom decided not to accept. "Well," Tom said. "It was nice running into you. But I'm in kind of a hurry." He pointed across the quad. "I was just going over to the snack bar for a quick cup of coffee. I've got hours of editing to do tonight."

"Why, what a nice idea," Celine said. "I have nowhere else to go. I'd love to have a coffee with you."

Nina was standing in the middle of Elizabeth's room, counting the open bags of food as she slowly revolved in place. "Pretzels . . . gourmet potato chips . . . Native American blue corn chips . . . pistachios . . . double-fudge cookies *with* walnuts . . . chocolate-covered raisins . . ." Nina groaned. "I love chocolate-covered raisins." She threw herself on Elizabeth's bed. "I don't know how can you stand it, Elizabeth. There's too much temptation. My fifteen-hundred-calorie-a-day diet wouldn't stand up to this kind of attack for more than ten minutes."

"You get used to it." Elizabeth laughed. "It's not that hard, really. I just keep reminding myself who bought the stuff, and my appetite disappears."

Nina shook her head. "What a twisted girl she is. She must spend a fortune on junk food trying to get you to go on a binge. Maybe we should take it downtown to the soup kitchen. I'm sure there are a lot of homeless people around who'd love these mesquite potato chips."

"When Celine starts leaving out fruit and vegetables, we'll take it down," Elizabeth said. "But for now I think we'll just let Celine waste her granny's money."

"Where is the Vampire Queen, anyway?" Nina asked, stretching out on the bed and resting her head on her arm. "Another big party?"

"Why, Nina Harper," Elizabeth said in mock-seriousness, "what a clever young woman you are. You must be at the top of your class."

Nina laughed. "Does Celine *ever* do any work?" she asked. It was hard for her to imagine not working all the time, as she herself did, but to do nothing at all was completely incomprehensible. Didn't Celine ever feel guilty? Didn't she ever worry that she wasn't going to make it in the big bad world? Didn't she get bored just having fun all the time?

"No." Elizabeth took two apples out of her desk and tossed one to her friend. "You never stop working, and the Queen of Darkness never starts."

She took a bite of her apple. "If we could just put a tiny bit of Celine into you, or a whole lot of you into Celine, we'd be well on our way to creating a normal person."

Nina watched Elizabeth for a few seconds, slowly chewing her apple. "You really think I work too hard?" she asked at last. "I mean, really?"

Elizabeth sat down beside Nina. "Of course I think you work too hard. You never seem to do anything just because you enjoy it."

"That's not true," Nina said defensively. "I enjoy my classes, Elizabeth. I really do. And I just can't have a good time doing something completely frivolous."

Elizabeth squeezed her arm. "I know you do, Nina. But there are other things besides classes."

Nina pulled something out of the pocket of her shirt. It was a pearl-gray sheet of paper, folded into quarters. "So do you think I should go to this?" she asked.

Elizabeth looked over her shoulder as Nina unfolded it. "What is it?" she asked. "It looks like an invitation."

"It is. The Black Students Union is having a big dinner in honor of Archie Springwater, the famous physicist."

"I didn't know Archie Springwater graduated from here," Elizabeth said, her eyes scanning the page. "That's so cool, isn't it? I mean, he's one of the most brilliant scientists in the space program."

She gave Nina a look. "And I didn't know you belonged to the BSU. Why have you been so quiet about it?"

Nina laughed. "Me be quiet? I wasn't being quiet, Elizabeth. I don't belong." She smiled shyly. "But I've been thinking about it. I mean, it is a good organization, isn't it? And I could learn a lot."

Elizabeth took the invitation from her hand. "It's an excellent organization," she agreed. "You could learn a lot *and* have a good time." She turned the invitation over. A knowing grin spread across her face. "What's this?" she demanded. She read the message written on the back of the BSU flyer. "If you don't come, I'm going to have no one to talk to, since I've already reserved the seat next to me for you. Besides, anyone as good at chemistry and physics as you are can't pass up an opportunity to meet this man. See you soon, Bryan."

Elizabeth looked up. "Bryan?" she asked. "Who's Bryan, Nina Harper? Have you been keeping secrets from me?"

Nina could feel her cheeks burning. "He's just this guy in my chemistry class," she said, taking back the invitation and folding it up again. "It's no big deal."

"Bryan?" Elizabeth repeated. "You couldn't possibly mean Bryan Nelson, boy genius, blues guitarist extraordinaire, and absolute hunk? *That* Bryan Nelson?"

Nina couldn't stop herself from grinning. "Well, as a matter of fact, that does sound like the same guy."

Elizabeth's blue-green eyes sparkled like the sea on a sunny day. "I can't believe you, Nina! Are you telling me that you would actually consider *not* going? Now I know you've been studying too hard."

"So you think I should go?" Nina asked. "You don't think I'd have more fun with my physics homework?"

"You'd better go," Elizabeth said with a laugh. "If you don't, I'll drag you there myself."

Nina pretended to consider this, her brow furrowed and her mouth in a frown. "All right," she said at last. "You win. I'll go." She looked over at the bowl beside her on the lamp table. "Maybe I'll have just three chocolate raisins to celebrate this momentous decision . . ."

Elizabeth gave her a warning look. "I wouldn't do that if I were you," she said.

Nina raised one eyebrow. "Why not? Are they stale?"

"No, they're not stale." A mischievous smile made the dimple in Elizabeth's left cheek appear. "They've been sprayed with Celine's perfume."

"What?" Nina laughed. "But who would do a thing like that?" she asked, playing dumb.

Elizabeth put on an innocent face and shrugged. "Who knows?"

*　　　*　　　*

Danny looked up from the book he was reading as Tom came into their room.

"Well, if it isn't my long-lost roommate, Thomas Workaholic Watts," he said. "I was wondering if I was ever going to see you again." He gave Tom a cynical grin. "You may have forgotten, but we were going to get some pizza about two hours ago." He put down his book. "Maybe you don't need food to exist, but I do. My stomach's really upset about the delay."

Tom threw his things on his bed and collapsed in the chair beside Danny's desk. "I'm sorry," he said. "I got started on this new story and I just couldn't stop."

"New story?" Danny echoed. "But you just finished the old story. I thought you were going to give up your Crusader Rabbit persona for a while." He looked at Tom out of the corner of his eye. Tom was pretending to be interested in the newspaper on Danny's desk. "Okay, what's this one about?"

Tom tore his attention away from an article on a dog that had walked two thousand miles to find its owner. He smiled. "Hazing," he said. "Fraternity hazing. Especially as practiced by such fraternities as the Sigmas."

Danny whistled, but didn't smile back. It seemed to him that for someone who liked to keep a low profile, Tom spent a lot of time laying himself on the line. "What is with you, man?" he

68

asked. "Are you really on some kind of mission, or is it that you just don't know when to quit? Crusader Rabbit's going to end up in somebody's stewpot if he isn't careful."

"I'm not on a big mission," Tom answered simply. "I just don't like unfairness, that's all. I want to find out the truth about these guys."

"Everybody says they're after truth," Danny mused. "You're the only person I know who breaks his neck trying to find it."

"Me and Elizabeth," Tom said.

"You and Elizabeth." Danny gave him a thoughtful look. "So, much to my and everyone else's amazement, Elizabeth Wakefield is working with you on this story?"

Tom stared back as though he didn't know what Danny was getting at. "Sure." He nodded. "Who else? She's the best reporter I've got. She's the most intelligent, the most resourceful, the—"

"Whoa, Tombo!" Danny held up his hands. "You don't have to convince me. I believe you." He studied Tom's face for a moment. "But I also believe that your interest in Ms. Wakefield is more than professional."

"Come on, Danny. Can't you—"

"Why don't you just go ahead and ask her out? Get it over with?" Danny asked. "The suspense is killing me. I feel like I'm living in a soap opera." He clasped his hands melodramatically. "Will Tom Watts ask Elizabeth Wakefield out on a date, or will he ask her twin sister by mistake? Which of them will say yes? Is Elizabeth really Elizabeth, or is she really her twin sister in disguise?"

Tom smiled sarcastically and folded his arms across his chest. "Very funny," he said. "Truly funny. But this isn't Daniel Haven't-Had-a-Date-since-September Wyatt giving me advice about women, is it?"

"At least I had a date in September," Danny said. "You haven't had a date in two years."

Danny noticed the shadow of pain that always appeared in Tom's eyes when the past was mentioned, but both of them pretended that it wasn't there.

"If you're such an expert on women, Wyatt, then what are you doing here with me? Why aren't you out having a grand old time with some beautiful girl?"

Danny got to his feet. "Because I feel sorry for you, that's why." He took his jacket off the back of his chair. "And besides, if it weren't for me, you'd never eat."

Tom got up, too. "Not pizza, though, Danny. You and I have already proved that an American male in his twenties can live on pizza. Let's get something else."

"Sure," Danny said. "We'll get a calzone instead."

"Eni—Alexandra!" Elizabeth couldn't hide her surprise.

She'd answered the door, expecting to find one

of Celine's friends wanting to borrow Celine's Thighmaster or battery charger as they always did. Instead there was Enid Rollins, her best friend from high school.

Only now, of course, Enid wasn't Enid anymore, she was Alexandra; and she wasn't Elizabeth's best friend, she hung out with the superjock crowd.

Recovering from the surprise of seeing Enid on her doorstep, Elizabeth stepped back. "Well, this is an unexpected visit." She laughed nervously. "Come on in." Elizabeth removed one of her roommate's sweaters from her armchair and tossed it on Celine's bed. "Sit down, Alex. Do you want a drink or something?" She pointed to the boxes of food around the room. "There's plenty to eat if you're hungry. Only, I don't recommend the chocolate raisins."

Enid didn't smile or respond. She stepped a few feet into the room, but she didn't sit down. She just stood there, looking serious and uncomfortable while Elizabeth chattered away, trying to fill up the cold space around them.

At last Enid's eyes met hers. She took a deep breath. "No thanks, Elizabeth. I don't want to sit down or anything." Enid took another deep breath. "This isn't really a social call."

Elizabeth remained standing, too. "No?" She smiled warily. It didn't feel like a social call—it felt more like a visit from the police.

"No." Enid shook her head, her eyes on the wall behind Elizabeth. She took an audible breath. "I came because of Tom Watts's broadcast," she blurted out. "Your and Tom's story, about the . . . the irregularities in the way athletes have been recruited on this campus?"

Elizabeth's stomach tightened. *Of course*. The sports story. How dumb could she be? Enid was going out with Mark Gathers, the biggest star on the basketball team. Elizabeth had been worried about Todd's being implicated in the scandal, but she hadn't really given much thought to Mark Gathers.

Enid's face was suffused with color, and her hands were clenched at her sides. "I just can't believe you did that, Elizabeth," she said, still looking at something behind Elizabeth. "I know you're upset about breaking up with Todd and everything, but I can't believe you could do something so spiteful."

"What are you talking about?" Elizabeth asked quietly. "I didn't write that story out of spite, Alex. I wrote it because it was true. Because what's been going on isn't right. Can't you see that?"

Enid's eyes filled with tears. "But it's right to betray your friends? It's right to take things I told you in confidence and spread them all over campus?"

Elizabeth could feel her own cheeks starting to burn. "I never betrayed any confidence, Alex," she said, forcing herself to remain calm. "There were things you told me that made me suspicious—about Mark not really worrying about studying, and the expensive restaurants he took you to, and the new Explorer he just got—and that made me ask myself some questions. But that's all. Then I went and found out the answers to those questions myself. And the answers suggest that what's been going on in the sports department isn't completely aboveboard and honest. People at this school have a right to know that."

"But what about Mark?" Enid demanded, suddenly hurling herself onto Elizabeth's bed. "What's going to happen to him, Elizabeth? Did you think of that before you started? Did you think about Todd? You could have ruined their careers." She swiped at her eyes with the back of her sleeve. "Not to mention my life."

Elizabeth's heart was racing. She'd thought it all through before she started investigating the sports department; she and Tom had discussed the implications several times. She'd even told Todd before she started, and he'd assured her he was clean. She'd made her decision—that the truth was the most important thing. Now, however, faced with Enid's tears and grief, she had to wonder. Had she been spiteful? Had she been insensitive? If it turned out that Mark and Todd were involved in the scandal, was it her fault?

And then she heard Tom's voice in her head.

You didn't ruin anybody's career, Elizabeth. People make their own choices in life, and then they have to live with the consequences.

"How about a cup of coffee, Alex?" Elizabeth said. "Maybe we can talk this through."

Enid sniffled back tears. "I don't think so, Elizabeth," she said in a choked voice. "I'm not sure I can ever talk to you again."

Chapter
Four

Jessica gave herself one last appraising glance in the mirror. She was wearing a pale-yellow sheath and her long, shimmering hair was clipped back with a silver barrette. She looked like a perfect Theta Alpha Theta pledge. The Thetas favored pastel colors and a certain preppy sophistication. Jessica picked up her bag and the note she'd written for Mike and hurriedly left the bedroom. She wanted to get out of the apartment before Mike got home, because she knew that if he looked at her with those pleading gold eyes and asked her not to go to the Theta party, she'd be tempted to stay.

"And you can't stay home tonight," she told herself severely. "You missed the last social. If you miss this one, you'll get kicked out of the sorority." The Thetas not only believed in pastels and sophistication, they believed in loyalty to your sisters above all else.

She propped her note on the kitchen table, where Mike would be sure to see it, and started toward the door. Before she could reach it, it swung open, and she saw what would on any other night be a wonderful vision: Mike with a bouquet of flowers in his arms.

"How's my baby?" he asked, not even bothering to shut the door behind him as he came up and took her in his arms. "I brought you some roses," he whispered. "Rose petals are the only thing I can think of that are as soft as your skin."

Jessica could feel herself melting. It would be so nice to kick off her shoes and spend the evening curled up on the couch with Mike, planning things they would do together. They would kiss and hug and feed each other pizza while they pretended to watch a video.

Mike pressed his lips to hers, surrounding her with his body. But instead of the explosion of fireworks she usually imagined when Mike kissed her like that, Jessica saw the face of Alison Quinn glaring at her disapprovingly.

"Oh, gosh," she gasped, pushing him away. "I've got to go, Mike. I'm going to be late."

"Late?" He grinned, pulling her toward him again. "Late for what? I'm going to make you my famous sweet-and-sour chicken tonight and beat you at backgammon."

"I can't tonight," Jessica said, wriggling free. "I've got a thing at the sorority house."

He looked down at her, pouting like a little boy. "Again? You just had a thing with the Thetas the other night."

Jessica sighed, but it was a sigh full of affection. "I know, Mike," she said, smiling impishly, "but if you remember, I didn't go."

He frowned. "You didn't? Are you sure?"

She hugged him tight. "Yes, I'm sure. So this time I have to go, or I'll be in big trouble."

He touched his lips to her hair. "Why don't you stay here where you'll be appreciated? I've been looking forward to being with you all day."

It took all her resolve not to give in. "I can't, Mike, I really can't." She stood on tiptoe and kissed his chin. "But I won't be late. I'll be home by nine thirty, I promise." This time she kissed his lips. "Maybe we could have that sweet-and-sour chicken then."

William White leaned his head against the back of the booth, his eyes on Celine. His gaze wasn't affectionate, Celine decided. It was more like being speared by icicles.

"You're sure?" he asked again. "You're absolutely sure?"

Celine tossed back her thick, unruly hair. "I'm as sure as I can be, sugar," she said. She smiled into his icy eyes, trying to disguise how tedious she was finding him. What did he want, a written guarantee? "I asked the Princess if she knew who her admirer was, and she said no." Celine shrugged. "I myself cannot understand how a woman could have no clue about a thing like that—I mean, that's the kind of thing a woman's *supposed* to know by instinct—but Elizabeth seems to have no idea."

His fingertips tapped out a tune on the tabletop.

She lifted her glass to her lips and took a delicate sip of iced coffee, her eyes narrowed and watchful. "But I can tell you who she wants it to be," Celine teased, as though this was the last thing William would want to know. "If that's of any interest to you."

The tune stopped abruptly.

It really was amazing, Celine thought, gazing at him. It was unnervingly easy to picture William with fangs; especially when he smiled like that.

"Who?"

She put down her glass with a discreet click. "Tom," she said softly. "Tom Watts."

"And do you think he wrote it?"

"It seems pretty likely, doesn't it?" Celine smiled sweetly. "After all, it wasn't you."

"No," William said, smiling back. "But it will be."

Everyone was laughing and talking at once, but no one was laughing or talking as much as Jessica Wakefield.

It was an amazing thing, considering how much Jessica had missed Mike on the drive to campus and the sorority house. *Maybe I should have stayed home after all,* she'd kept telling herself. *Am I crazy, leaving the most beautiful man in the world all alone so I can hang out with a bunch of girls?* She'd thought of how cute Mike was when he was cooking, and how grumpy he got if he was right in the middle of something tricky like making the sauce and she tried to kiss him. At one point, imagining him holding out the spoon for her to take a taste, she'd almost turned the Karmann Ghia back toward home, but Alison Quinn's haughty face had reappeared in her mind, scowling of course, so Jessica stayed where she was. *It's only one night,* she'd consoled herself. *We both managed to exist years without each other before we met, so we can make it through a couple of hours.*

But now that she was here, she was having a wonderful time. She'd forgotten how much fun she used to have with Isabella and Denise and her other friends in the days before Michael McAllery. She'd almost forgotten why she'd wanted to join the Thetas in the first place. But now she remembered—so she'd have a group of girls to hang out with who liked the same things she liked and knew how to have a good time.

"Whose turn is next?" one of the Thetas shouted out. They'd been playing an informal game of Truth or Dare while they ate cookies and listened to music. "One of the pledges has to go next."

Magda Helperin, the president of Theta Alpha

Theta, smiled regally. "How about Jessica?"

"Sure," Jessica said brightly. She flicked her golden hair over her shoulder. She knew that Magda wasn't asking her a question, she was giving her an order. Jessica raised her head high and stuck out her chin. "Ask me anything," she said. "I, a loyal Theta Alpha Theta pledge, promise to tell the complete truth."

Alison, sitting on the other side of the room from Magda, made herself more comfortable in her chair. "I have a truth or dare for our little sister," she said. She paused for a few seconds, smoothing the cuff of her crisp, starchy white blouse. She smiled as though she were about to do something everyone should be really impressed with. "Tell us, Jessica," Alison purred, "was it really Elizabeth who went to the Homecoming game with Peter Wilbourne III, as you said, or was it you?"

Over the years, Jessica had gotten herself into more than one tight corner. Sometimes she had had to lie her way out. Sometimes she had had to bluff. Now and then she had even had to tell the truth. But she had learned how to think quickly, and to judge just which method she should choose.

Jessica looked at Alison's face, her own face as blank as a newly plastered wall. Should she lie, bluff, or tell the truth? Alison smiled at her. It was a small, encouraging smile, but it was enough to tell Jessica what she needed to know. Alison knew the truth. Jessica could see it in her sparkling eyes. Somehow or other, she had guessed or she had found out, but she definitely knew that the twin kissing the loathsome Peter Wilbourne in the bleachers during halftime that afternoon wasn't Elizabeth Wakefield.

"I cannot tell a lie," Jessica said. "It wasn't Elizabeth, it was me." She made a helpless gesture with her arms. "What could I do? I was desperate to join the Thetas, and Elizabeth wouldn't help me." She shook her head. "Real sisters aren't half as loyal as sorority sisters," she added.

Isabella and Denise led the laughter, and even Magda joined in.

"I'll say one thing for you, Jess," the Theta president told her, obviously not displeased, "you have a lot of spirit. That's what we like to see in a Theta. A lot of spirit and fight."

"It's a good thing you're such a talented actress," Alison said. "You fooled everyone, including Peter himself." She made herself a little more comfortable in her chair. "One more question, Jess?"

Jessica shrugged. "Sure."

"Are you dating anyone seriously yet?" She smiled again. "You know, anyone special?"

Jessica knew that the Thetas didn't approve of Mike, which was why she'd been careful about keeping her relationship with him a secret. As far as the Thetas were concerned, Jessica still lived in a

81

dorm with Isabella. Isabella might not approve of Mike either, but she would never give Jessica away.

"Well?" prompted Alison. "Don't tell me you can't remember."

Jessica was tempted to tell the truth. Why should she lie to her sorority sisters—especially about something as important as the man she loved? She glanced over at Isabella. The look in Isabella's eyes was as easy to read as a billboard on the highway. *Don't tell the truth,* it said. *You can get away with it. Don't tell the truth.*

Jessica turned back to Alison with a laugh. "The thing I can't remember is who I went out with last." She rolled her eyes. "I mean, there are so many gorgeous guys on this campus, who can keep track?"

"It's not a problem everyone has," Denise Waters called out, with a smile in Jessica's direction.

Jessica smiled back. *It sure is a good thing I'm such a talented actress,* she thought. She caught Isabella's eye again, and she knew Isabella was thinking the very same thing.

Winston and the other Sigma plebes stood in a silent row that stretched from one side of the dark, dank basement of the fraternity house to the other. Winston managed not to yelp as something with many more than four legs ran over his foot. *Whatever you do, don't make a noise,* he told himself. *Don't show fear.*

Hazing hadn't been going on that long, but Winston had already figured out that his fraternity brothers were a lot like sharks: they sensed fear. Also like sharks, as soon as they sensed fear they got ready to attack.

Someone at the end of the row sneezed, breaking the tense silence.

"Were you given permission to make a sound, little brother?" a voice shouted from across the room.

"I—No—" the unhappy plebe began in a whisper.

"Then don't make any until you're given permission," the voice ordered. It laughed unpleasantly. "Or you'll be very sorry you did."

Winston said a silent prayer that he wouldn't have to sneeze, burp, cough, or even breathe too loudly until this ordeal was over. After the scene with Peter Wilbourne when he caught Winston talking to Elizabeth, Winston was pretty sure he wouldn't get off with just a warning. If he'd had any doubts about how popular he was with the Sigma president, they were gone. Peter Wilbourne hated him. He was sure of that. What Winston couldn't figure out was why the Sigmas had pledged him anyway.

The guy next to Winston shifted from one foot to the other.

"Don't move!" the same voice bellowed. "You know the rules."

Winston fought back a sigh. The only possible good thing about this evening as far as he could see was that neither Denise Waters nor Elizabeth Wakefield was here to see it. Not that there was really any big deal about a bunch of freshmen standing in a basement, if you thought about it, Winston told himself. After all, there were probably guys all over the country standing in basements right at that moment. Guys in Washington State. Guys in Arizona, Texas, Wisconsin, Missouri, Alabama, even Alaska. Winston shuddered. He was grateful he was in California and not Alaska, that was for sure. Because the guys in Sigma house, at least, were all stripped down to their underwear.

Suddenly, there was a blaze of light so bright it was almost blinding. Winston shut his eyes as he and his fellow little brothers were hosed down with ice-cold water.

Don't make a sound, Winston warned himself. *Don't shiver. If you shiver, they'll hear you. Then they'll probably drown you.*

The basement was pitched into darkness again. It was so quiet, Winston could hear his heart pounding and feel the goose bumps rising on his flesh.

The lights went on again. Something cold and wet fell over the heads and bodies of the plebes. His eyes were trying to adjust to the sudden light, and it took Winston a second to realize that it wasn't water this time. It was a dark-red, sticky liquid.

Oh no, Winston thought. *It's blood. They're cov-*

ering us in blood. He bit down on his tongue. Whatever happened, he couldn't throw up.

"This is the blood of Ned Searles, the plebe who couldn't take it last year," boomed the same voice. "Do any of you want to be this year's Ned Searles?"

"No, sir!" Winston and the other plebes shouted with feeling.

A little of the sticky liquid trickled into Winston's mouth. *Punch,* he thought, almost collapsing with relief. *It's only punch!* And then, although Sigma plebes were forbidden from doing too much thinking, a thought occurred to him. *I'm punch drunk,* he thought, giggling a little in spite of himself.

The second giggle had barely left his throat when Peter Wilbourne and his two best buddies appeared in front of him.

"What's so funny, boy?" Peter demanded. "Is there something so funny that it would make you break a Sigma rule?"

"I'm sorry, sir," Winston mumbled. He swallowed hard. "It's just that . . . I was thinking . . . the punch and everything . . . well, I was thinking that I'm punch drunk . . ."

Much to Winston's surprise, a few little laughs escaped from the other shivering plebes.

Winston started to smile.

"I'd wipe that stupid grin off my face if I were you, boy," Peter Wilbourne growled.

Winston wiped the stupid grin off his face, his heart sinking somewhere below his feet. He was in trouble now. He could tell.

Peter Wilbourne leered. "Tonight," the Sigma president announced, "as punishment for breaking the rule of silence, plebe Egbert is going to sleep down here." He put his face close to Winston's and gave him the biggest smile Winston had ever seen. "With all our insect friends. And the goat."

"I guess it's pretty much what we should have expected," Tom said as he and Elizabeth left the television studio together. "But I'm still sorry it happened."

Elizabeth gave him a rueful smile. "I'm sorry it happened, too," she said. "Alex was so incredibly upset. And so angry." She waited while he locked the door behind them. "We used to be best friends. Now she thinks I made up the whole story just because I'm mad at her."

Tom fell into step beside her. "That's not what she thinks, Elizabeth," he reassured her. "She's probably afraid that her boyfriend—what's his name?"

"Mark Gathers."

Tom nodded. "Right, the basketball prince. Well, she's probably afraid that he really is going to be incriminated in the whole thing, so she's taking it out on you."

The smile Elizabeth gave him was full of gratitude. After Enid had left her room earlier,

Elizabeth felt like crying—crying or eating some of Celine's potato chips, she couldn't decide. Instead, she'd gone to see Tom. It had been the right decision. As usual, talking things over with him put everything into perspective.

"I know you're right," Elizabeth said with a sigh. "Thanks. I feel much better." She shook her head. "This tough-reporter business isn't always easy, is it?"

Tom stuck his hands in his pockets, looking straight ahead. "Sometimes I don't think anything's easy," he said in a low voice. "That's why you've got to be sure that what you go for is worth it."

"You mean like the hazing story?" Elizabeth asked.

He nodded. "Yeah, like the hazing story."

His shoulder brushed against hers as they walked. Elizabeth felt a small thrill of electricity run down her arm. Resisting the temptation to move closer, she moved away.

"These fraternity guys think they're really big men," Tom was saying. "They think they can do whatever they want."

"I'll start checking out the microfiche in the library tomorrow," Elizabeth said. "You know, see what hazing stories I can find from the past. But I think maybe you're going to have to be the one to talk with Winston. He won't even speak to me on the phone since Peter Wilbourne caught us together."

"Sure," Tom agreed. "I'll talk to him." He smiled to himself. "Peter Wilbourne III is not one of my favorite people. It'd be a pleasure to get the goods on him."

They came to the fork in the path and stopped. Elizabeth would go left to reach her dorm; Tom would go right to get to his.

She was suddenly aware that it was a warm, still night. Above them, a yellow moon as round as a ball seemed to be floating in a spangled sky.

"Well . . ." Elizabeth said.

"Well . . ." Tom said.

She looked into his eyes. Sometimes they were cold and guarded, but tonight they were open and warm. Tonight they were looking at her in the way she sometimes dreamed they would. It was on the tip of her tongue to ask him about the poem. *Go ahead,* she urged herself. *Ask him. It had to be him, it had to.* She opened her mouth, the words forming themselves on her lips.

"Tom!"

Both Tom and Elizabeth looked up. Celine was hurrying down the path toward them. Nodding dismissively at Elizabeth, Celine looked at Tom. "Which way are you going?" she asked. "I have to go over to Wagoner Hall. Maybe I could go part of the way with you?"

Tom looked from Celine back to Elizabeth. "I . . . um . . ."

"I'd better get going," Elizabeth said, starting

88

to hurry away. "I've got a lot to do tonight."

"See you later, Lizzie," Celine called. "Don't wait up."

Jessica pulled into the parking lot of her apartment building and practically threw herself out of the car. It was already after ten. She'd told Mike she'd be home by nine thirty, but the evening had gone on and on and she couldn't get away. Every time she made a move to leave, Alison Quinn gave her a suspicious "Where do you think you're going in such a hurry?" look, and Jessica had sat back down, pretending she had nothing better to do than eat cookies and gossip.

She was almost at the entrance to the building when a handsome, laughing couple stepped out. Jessica froze, looking around for someplace to hide. *I don't believe this,* she said to herself. *Why me? Why now?*

Seeing her only feet in front of them, the couple froze too. Steven stopped laughing so abruptly, it was as though someone had pulled out his plug.

Billie glanced warily at Steven, but smiled at Jessica. "Hi, Jess," she said. She put her arm through Steven's. "We were just going to get a bite to eat. Late classes."

"Hi, Billie." Jessica smiled back. Thank goodness for her brother's girlfriend. She was giving her a chance to escape. "Hi, Steven." She nodded in his direction as she tried to get past them.

"Not so fast, Jess," Steven said. He shook himself free from Billie and stepped in Jessica's path. "There are a couple of things we need to talk about."

Jessica groaned inwardly. It was bad enough when her father used that tone of voice, but to have her brother putting on his lecture voice was too much.

She pushed past him. "Not tonight, Steven. Please? It's late, and I'm tired, and I haven't had dinner yet either."

He grabbed her by the arm and hauled her back. "Never mind dinner," Steven said. "This is important."

Billie leaned against the building. "Steven," she said wearily, "I agree with Jessica. Why don't you wait till tomorrow?"

"I'm not going to start shouting or anything," Steven said reasonably. "I just want to make a few things clear."

Jessica bit her lip. "You've already made a few things clear," she said, trying to pull out of his grasp. "You don't like Mike. You don't like me living with Mike. And you don't like Mike. What else is there to say?"

"There's plenty," Steven said, his voice already beginning to rise. "The man's a bum, Jess. He drinks, he runs around with women, who knows how he makes all his money—"

Jessica held up her hand. "Fine," she said. "Great. Now I know. Thank you, big brother, for telling me." She made a bored face. "Can I go get my dinner now? My boyfriend's waiting for me."

"No, you cannot go running to your boyfriend. I'm not finished," Steven said through gritted teeth. "Look, I thought I'd give you a little time playing house with that idiot to come to your senses." He glared over at Billie. "Some people thought that was the best way to handle the situation, to let you find out for yourself what a mistake you were making."

Jessica gave him an arrogant look. "But I'm not making a mistake," she said coolly. "Moving in with Mike is the best thing I've ever done."

"Sure you think that," Steven argued. "You're young and impressionable, so you think Mike McAllery is the best thing since microwave pizza. But he isn't, Jess. He's going to hurt you."

"Well, that's my problem, isn't it?" Jessica snapped, yanking herself from his grasp. "Not yours."

He stepped in front of her. "No. It is my problem. I'm your older brother. Mom and Dad expect me to keep an eye on you. I can't sit around doing nothing while you shack up with the first piece of garbage you stumble across."

Jessica wanted to hit him. He was so hypocritical, so unfair. Steven and Billie were living together because they were in love. But when it came to her and Mike, it wasn't love anymore, it was shacking up. It was unfair and untrue.

"Is that a threat?" Jessica shouted back. "Is it?"

"If you want to look at it like that," Steven said. "If you don't move back to the dorm, I can't see that I have any choice but to tell them what's going on."

Billie sighed.

"Oh, really?" Jessica thundered. "You have no choice?" She looked from her brother to Billie. "Well, go ahead and tell them, you hypocrite. I don't care what you do!" She shoved him as she ran through the door.

All Jessica wanted to do was get inside her apartment and throw herself into Mike's strong arms. Tears of rage streaming down her face, Jessica took the stairs two at a time.

"Mike!" she called as she flung herself into the apartment. "Mike!"

She ran into the living room and stopped. There was no music playing, no smell of sweet-and-sour chicken simmering, no sound at all.

"Mike!" she called again. But she already knew the truth. Mike wasn't home.

Nina was just coming out of the pay phone in the lounge when Elizabeth got back to the dorm.

"Are you okay?" Elizabeth asked as they headed toward their floor. "You look like you got some bad news."

Nina shook her head. "Not really. I just talked

to my mother." She rolled her eyes. "She got on my case a little."

"Got on your case?" Elizabeth looked at her in surprise. "What could she possibly get on your case for? You're a mother's dream. You're a straight-A student, totally responsible and mature, you don't run around, or drink, or cut classes—"

"You want to know what it was?" Nina asked. She made a face. "It was because I said I was going to the BSU dinner."

Elizabeth looked over at Nina, wondering if she'd misheard her. "Your mother's unhappy because you're going to the BSU dinner?"

"Uh-huh. She wants to know why I feel I have to go to something like that."

Elizabeth looked perplexed. "But your mom is black, right?" she asked.

Nina grinned. "Oh, yeah, she's black. So is my father." She put her arm around Elizabeth as they turned onto their floor. "That's where I get this dark skin from."

"So what's the problem?"

Nina shrugged. "My parents don't believe in rocking the boat. They got where they are by working harder than anybody else, and they think that's what I should do."

"That is what you do," Elizabeth said.

"I know," Nina said, "but my mother thinks that's all I should do. She thinks the BSU is too radical, and that I shouldn't need an organization like that. She thinks it's only for people who can't make it on their own or who want to complain or blame everybody else for their failures."

"That's crazy!" Elizabeth said. "Besides, you're only going to a dinner. You—" The words vanished from her mind as she stared at the door to her room.

Nina whistled. "What's larger than a poem, more expensive than a poem, and standing outside your door?" she asked.

"Two dozen white roses," Elizabeth said, trying to take it all in. Her mind went back to the tiny white rose William White had given her that night in the library weeks ago.

"Does this mean we know who your secret admirer is?" Nina asked.

Elizabeth nodded. "Yes," she answered, trying to keep the disappointment out of her voice. "Yes, I guess it does."

Chapter
Five

It wasn't easy being a man, Winston thought as he limped across the Sweet Valley University campus. Men had to prove themselves. Look at Hercules. Look at Ulysses. Look at Daniel Boone and Davy Crockett.

"Look at *me*," Winston told himself as he hobbled down the lawn toward Oakley Hall. "I'm going through a male rite of passage. Just like the Indians used to do."

Slowly, and with a certain amount of agony, he made his way to the back entrance. At least it was early. With a little luck, he'd be able to get safely inside without being seen. Winston was too tired and in too much pain from trying to sleep on a concrete floor in his underwear covered with sticky red stuff to actually have a plan, but he did have a vague idea that he would sneak into his dorm, take a shower, and maybe even catch a short nap on a bed with blankets, pillows, and a mattress before his first class.

Winston opened the door to Oakley Hall and stuck his head in. There was no one in sight. Just the smell of the hallway made him feel weak with relief. Oakley Hall smelled of the things he'd come to associate with women: makeup and perfumes, soaps and shampoos, cookies and yogurt. He could hear radios playing and the comforting sound of female conversation and laughter. *Home,* Winston thought. *It's good to be home.*

It wasn't easy to tiptoe, because of his back, but Winston did the best he could, holding his breath as he shuffled toward his door. He fumbled in his pocket for the key.

"What happened to you?"

It was Denise Waters. Of all the girls in the world, the one Winston didn't want to see him looking like this was Denise.

"Nothing," Winston lied, keeping his back to her and the pain out of his voice as he tried to make the key fit into the lock. "I just had a late night."

"A late night?" She laughed, but she sounded concerned. "Winnie, it's seven in the morning."

What was wrong with the key? Had the Sigmas changed his key while they'd had his clothes? He wouldn't put it past them.

"Winston," Denise said. "Turn around."

"I'm in a hurry, Denise." At least that was true.

He was in an incredible hurry. He had to get into his room before she got a really good look at him. Only, the key wouldn't open the stupid door.

"Turn around, Winnie. Or I'm coming after you. Let's not forget who beat you at arm wrestling the other night twenty-two times out of twenty-five."

Winston turned around.

Denise screamed.

"You're bleeding!" she shrieked, looking up and down the hall for help. "You're covered in blood!" She took hold of him, gently but firmly. "Have you been stabbed?" she asked, her beautiful eyes troubled and frightened. "Did you have an accident? Did someone run you over?" Her fingers lightly touched his face and neck, looking for wounds. "Winnie! Tell me what happened!"

As much as he didn't want Denise to take her hands away from him, Winston had to stop her. Doors were opening up and down the corridor. Girls in T-shirts and bathrobes were racing toward them, shouting.

Maia, the dorm monitor, came out of the room next to Winston's. "I'll call a doctor!" she said in her brisk, efficient way as soon as she saw Winston. "And the campus police!"

"No, please!" Winston held up his arms, wincing as the sudden movement caused his spine to seize. "I'm all right. Really. I'm not hurt. It's not blood."

"But you're all red," Debbie said, skidding to a stop beside him. "And you're filthy."

"You're obviously in pain," Denise said. "Look at you, you can hardly stand."

It was true, Winston realized. He could hardly stand. If he weren't holding on to the wall, he would probably fall over. "I'm fine, really," he said. "I spent the night at the fraternity house, that's all."

There was a communal groan. "Oh," the girls said together. "He was at the fraternity house."

Anoushka sniffed the air. "If you were at the fraternity house all night, what's that smell?" she wanted to know.

"Goat," Winston answered.

"You spent the night with a goat?" Maia demanded.

Winston nodded.

Denise took the key from his hand and unlocked his door. "I'll bet the goat looks better than you do," she said.

Usually, when Elizabeth was getting involved in a story, it was the most important thing on her mind. She'd dream about it. When she woke up, it would be the first thing she'd think of.

But the night before, Elizabeth had dreamt about the roses. She dreamt that she carried them across the campus to give them back to William White. She'd found him sitting in a study carrel in the library, reading a book about Byron.

William, she'd said to him in her dream. *I can't accept these. I really can't. Todd and I just broke up, you know. I'm not ready to start dating again.* White petals drifted onto the floor and shelves of the library. Petals floated onto the book about Byron.

William wouldn't take the roses back. He kept asking if she wanted more flowers. Did she want three dozen? Four dozen? Five? Six? He would buy her every rose in the world, if she wanted. *I bet Wilkins never gave you flowers like this,* William had said.

Then Tom came into the library, reciting the poem. He walked to her across the fallen petals as though he were walking through snow. *Did Todd ever write you a poem like this?* Tom asked her. *Anybody can give you flowers, but who else would write you a poem?*

It was that last part Elizabeth thought of when she woke up from the dream in the morning. *It's true. Just because William sent the roses doesn't mean that Tom didn't write the poem,* she told herself.

Elizabeth opened her eyes. The night before, when she and Nina found the roses outside her door, she couldn't hide her disappointment. Not that she wasn't happy to be given such a beautiful present. She was flattered and pleased by the attention. But as handsome, interesting, and charming as William White was—and as undeniably attracted as Elizabeth was to him—the sight of the roses had made her realize how much she'd wanted the writer of the poem to be Tom. She'd once again been sure it was Tom, convinced by her heart.

She sat up and looked around the room. The two dozen white flowers were crowding everything else on her desk. In the early-morning sunshine their petals almost seemed to glow; they looked too perfect to be real. Elizabeth smiled at the roses. *Tom could still have written the poem,* she told herself again.

Celine, sprawled across her rose-colored satin sheets, was snoring gently. Elizabeth looked over at her. She smiled to herself. The one thing didn't have to have anything to do with the other. She'd been silly to think it had.

Humming happily, Elizabeth jumped out of bed and grabbed her shower things from her dresser. It looked like it was going to be a very good day.

Nina was walking to her chemistry class, her mind on the conversation she'd had with her mother on the telephone the night before, when she sensed someone falling into step beside her.

"A buck fifty for your thoughts," said a deep male voice. "Two bucks, if you'll have a coffee with me after class."

Nina looked over and into Bryan Nelson's world-class smile. Her mother probably wouldn't approve of Bryan's hair, she decided. What was fashion statement on Nina's part was a political statement on Bryan's. Her mother certainly wouldn't approve of his African shirt or the single gold hoop in his ear. Nina's mother believed in blending in, not standing out. In fact, it had taken eight months to convince her to let Nina have her hair braided, and then she only gave in because Nina's grandmother sided with Nina.

She smiled back. "I don't think my thoughts are worth two bucks."

"Just so long as you aren't thinking about changing your mind about going to the BSU dinner with me," Bryan said. "That's all I ask."

Nina frowned.

He stopped, gently taking her arm to stop her, too. "Hey, I was joking." His beautiful hazel eyes searched her face. "You aren't thinking of backing out, are you?"

"No, of course not." Nina shook her head adamantly, but those eyes were very disturbing. "I mean, no, of course not. I'm really looking forward to it . . ."

He made a worried face. "What's wrong, then?"

"It's nothing, really." She started walking again. "Well, actually," she went on with a little sigh, "I talked to my mom last night and she wasn't too happy about me getting involved with the BSU."

Bryan laughed. His laugh was almost as spectacular as his smile. "Oh, is that all." He looked over, grinning. "She sounds like my father. He practically lost his breakfast when I told him I'd joined."

Nina felt as though a fifty-pound backpack had been taken from her shoulders. "He's afraid it's too radical, too, huh?"

Bryan's braids swung back and forth. "No, that's not it. He thinks it's too establishment. He thinks it's secretly run by whites."

"You're joking, right?" she asked with a laugh. "Your father doesn't really think the BSU is too establishment?"

"I'm not joking." Bryan swung around so he was walking backward in front of her. "My dad was one of those sixties radicals. He marched all over the South, rode buses, got thrown in jail for sitting down in all-white diners." The smile dimmed. "One of his best friends died in Mississippi, and he's never forgotten that. Or forgiven it." He shrugged and grinned again. "Sometime we'll get the film of the March on Washington out of the library archives, and I'll show you my dad. First you see him giving this speech, and then later you see him being carted off to jail."

Nina wasn't sure what to say. Her parents admired Martin Luther King, of course. But they hadn't marched on Washington. They were too busy working to pay for graduate school. "I'd like to see it," she said at last. "The film, I mean. And your father." She looked over as Bryan started to walk beside her again. "You must be proud of him."

"I am," he answered simply. "He's a solid man." He made a face. "I'm not so sure he's that proud of me, though. He thinks I'm too conservative."

"*You?*" Nina didn't even try to hide her astonishment. "My mother wouldn't think you're conservative. My mother would think you're practically a revolutionary."

Bryan nodded, his expression suddenly serious. "Oh, I am," he said. "That's why I invited you to a formal sit-down dinner. It's part of my cover." They stopped outside the chemistry classroom. "Is my cover working?" he asked her, his eyes sparkling with humor. "Are you still coming with me?"

She pretended to be considering this. "Yeah, it's working." She grinned. "So far."

Jessica was thinking about Mike as she walked into the bank. Which wasn't that surprising. She'd been thinking about Mike all morning. When her English teacher asked her a question on the book they were discussing, Jessica had answered, "Moby *who?*" Although, considering the state she was in, it was a miracle that she had answered at all.

She went to the unoccupied teller and pushed her withdrawal slip through the cage.

The night before, Jessica had sat on the sofa and cried about her fight with Steven and the fact that Mike hadn't come home until nearly midnight, and then, exhausted, she'd finally gone to bed.

When she got up in the morning, Mike was sound asleep on the couch, but he'd looked so peaceful that she hadn't wanted to wake him. Besides, what happened last night was her fault more than his. She was the one who was late; she was the one who left him to be with her friends.

Uncomprehending, Jessica watched the withdrawal slip slide back across the counter to her. She pushed it back. "No," she explained, trying not to sound impatient. "I want to cash it."

The teller didn't smile. "I'm sorry," the woman said, "but I can't cash it. There are insufficient funds in your account to cover this."

Why is this happening to me? Jessica wondered, staring back at the teller's impassive face. *First last night, and now this.*

"Insufficient funds?" she repeated. "But that's impossible." She was supposed to have enough money in the account to last until the end of the first semester, when her parents would put more in. They were nowhere near the end of the semester yet.

The teller wrote something on a piece of paper and shoved it under the grille. Jessica picked it up. Fifty-five cents. That was what she had in her account. Fifty-five cents to get her from now to the end of the term. Fifty-five cents wasn't going to get her from now to dinner.

"If you don't mind," the teller prompted, "there

104

are other customers. You're holding up the line."

Jessica nodded numbly. Numbly, she left the bank and stepped into the sunshine. It must have been moving in with Mike; there was no other explanation. She had bought a few things for the apartment to make it feel more like theirs than just his. And, of course, she had had to buy some new clothes. No one could expect her to live with a man with Mike's taste and style in her old clothes. But besides those few necessities, she'd tried to be careful. Mike refused to take any rent from her, but they had agreed to share the food and the telephone bill. *I guess I just didn't realize how expensive food and the telephone are*, she thought. When she'd lived at home and in the dorm, she'd tended to think of food and the telephone as free, like the air.

Now what? she asked herself. She couldn't go to her parents for more money, or they'd be sure to find out about Mike. She couldn't go to Steven, that was for sure. And she didn't want to tell Mike what had happened. But she couldn't survive without money.

Jessica frowned at the sidewalk, searching for some inspiration. She could ask Isabella, but she had the feeling that Isabella wouldn't be too sympathetic. She looked up at a store window with a sigh. Looking back at her was a pretty girl with long blond hair.

"Elizabeth!" Jessica cried out loud. Elizabeth

always had money. She never went on dates or anything like that, so of course she had money. She had nothing to spend it on.

She checked her watch. Elizabeth was sure to be in a class right now, and Jessica couldn't wait. She wanted to make a special dinner for Mike tonight to make up for yesterday. But she wasn't going to make him much of a meal with fifty-five cents.

There was only one thing she could do. *I'll just have to pretend to be Elizabeth and take what I need from her account,* Jessica decided. It was lucky that when they opened their college accounts, they'd joked about how close the numbers were, or she might not have remembered it.

Still looking in the window of the clothes shop, Jessica fished an elastic band from her pocket and put up her hair. Then she took off her sweater and jammed it into her book bag. She smiled at her reflection.

"How much money are you going to take out, Elizabeth?" she asked it. "Twenty? Thirty? Fifty?" She smiled at the window, and Elizabeth smiled back. It was a good thing she'd learned to copy her sister's handwriting at an early age, too.

Elizabeth leaned back in the chair of the microfiche carrel in the library and stretched her arms. The clock on the wall said six o'clock. She could hardly believe it. She'd been going through old editions of the school and local paper since after lunch, but she'd found so much stuff there that it felt as though only an hour had passed. She rubbed her eyes. No wonder she was feeling tired. Tired but exhilarated. *Wait'll Tom sees this,* she thought. *He's going to be as excited as I am.*

She looked at the pages of notes piled in front of her. Tom's hunch about hazing had even more substance than Elizabeth had imagined or Tom could have hoped for. There were dozens of letters from parents and town residents complaining about the hazing ritual, describing it as childish at best and dangerous at worst. There were dozens of articles by fraternity alumni and university spokesmen defending the tradition and explaining it away as no more than "harmless fun." For all of that, though, there were also reports of suspicious incidents, accidents, and even deaths going back to the fifties.

"Harmless fun, huh," Elizabeth mumbled to herself as she got her things together.

She knew she had something, but she wasn't quite sure what. There were bound to be patterns, but there was too much material for her to sort through now. The best thing to do would be to show Tom what she had. Maybe they could look through her notes together. A smile lit up her tired eyes. Yes, she decided, that was what she'd do. She'd bring what she'd found to the studio and they could analyze it together.

Elizabeth stopped, about to push in her chair,

gazing into space as another thought occurred to her. Maybe she'd have the opportunity to bring up the poem. She could quote a line from it, or even just introduce the subject of writing poetry, to see how he reacted.

Elizabeth picked up her backpack and headed out of the library, half her brain going through all the articles she'd read in the last few hours and the other half trying to come up with the best way to introduce the subject of poetry to Tom Watts.

"Once I thought that all I had was mine; that what was mine would always be . . ."

Elizabeth froze at the top of the library stairs. *That's from the poem,* she thought, *that's a line from the poem.* Her heart was galloping. She looked around, expecting to see Tom standing behind her.

But it wasn't Tom. If she'd thought about it, she would have known it wasn't Tom. The voice that recited that line didn't belong to him; it belonged to William White. William White, who was standing in the doorway only inches away. He was all in black and holding a white rose in his hand, as though he were a magician just pulling it from the air.

Unable to take her eyes from his, she stumbled for the right words. "I—I don't know what to say," she began. "I mean, thank you. Thank you for everything. For the flowers . . . for the poem . . ."

He touched the rose to her lips. "Thank *you*,"

he said. "You're the one who deserves the thanks."

"Why?"

"For being so beautiful," he said, tucking the flower into her hand. He smiled. "And for having dinner with me tomorrow night."

Elizabeth looked down at the delicate rose, wondering whether to accept or not. She looked back to William—still unsure of what to say.

But William was gone.

"Well," Elizabeth muttered to herself as she continued on her way to WSVU, "I guess that means I said yes."

Tom had just come back into his office with a Coke and a bag of potato chips—the snack that was going to allow him to work for a couple more hours without dying of hunger—when he heard footsteps coming down the hallway outside.

Please, he prayed silently. *Don't let it be that girl.* He looked around, wondering if he should hide. There was the storage closet, and there were several desks he could duck behind. The footsteps were getting closer and closer. It was definitely a woman. *I can't stand another half hour trapped with her. It's like some kind of torture.* The first time—the time Celine invited herself to the snack bar with him—had been bad enough. She'd gone on and on about her wealthy family and what it was like growing up in the South and all the fantastic parties she'd been to, until he'd had to fight with himself not to accidentally spill his coffee in her lap. But at least there had been other people around.

Last night, when she'd suddenly appeared like some kind of evil spirit and dragged him away just as he was trying to get up the courage to ask Elizabeth to go out to dinner with him, there hadn't been anyone else around. Just he and Celine, walking side by side to the other end of the campus. He'd rather have walked across the Mojave, barefoot. How did Elizabeth stand living in the same room with Celine? Tom was having enough trouble dealing with the fact that she was on the same campus he was.

The footsteps stopped outside his door, just as he knew they would. He caught his breath. It was too late. The doorknob began to turn. He'd waited too long, and now he couldn't hide. Still not breathing, Tom leaned against the wall and closed his eyes.

"What are you doing pressed into the corner, Tom? You look like you're playing hide-and-seek."

He opened his eyes. Elizabeth's voice was always music to his ears, but right now it sounded like a heavenly choir.

"It's you!" he cried, so relieved he forgot for once to hide his feelings. "I'm so glad it's you!"

Blushing a little, Elizabeth strode past him and dumped her things on his desk. "You're going to be even more glad when you see what I found," she said, pulling her notebook out of her backpack.

All worries about Celine forgotten, Tom hurried over to join Elizabeth. "You mean for the hazing story?" he asked. "You think you've got something?"

Elizabeth nodded. "I know I've got something." She opened her book. "I've made notes of all the papers and issues that had anything to do with hazing, going back to '53," she told him as he started to read one of the articles. "But I've also made copies of a couple of the more interesting ones." She watched him as he turned the page. "The trouble is, I'm not sure what exactly I've got."

"You mean you think there's a pattern, but you haven't worked out what it is yet?" he asked, not looking up.

"Exactly." She leaned close as he turned another page. "There was so much that my head's kind of spinning. I couldn't take it all in."

Tom read the caption of one of the stories out loud. "'Boys Will Be Boys.'" He gave a low whistle, unable to believe what he was reading as he got further into the story. He turned to Elizabeth in astonishment. "This is about a death," he said. "Somebody died."

"He isn't the only one." She flipped to the back of her notebook. "Look," she ordered. "I've written down the statistics of accidents and deaths over the last four decades."

Tom ran his finger down the columns, silent as he concentrated. "You know, it looks as though

111

there's been a death due to hazing at least every seven years since the mid-fifties."

The golden head beside him nodded. "I'm not sure that that's the worst part," Elizabeth said, her voice little more than a whisper.

"No?" Tom asked. "What's the worst part?"

She looked up, her eyes the color of a troubled sea. "The worst part is that the last death happened exactly seven years ago."

All right, here's the deal, Jessica was saying to herself as she pulled the Karmann Ghia into the parking lot of her building. *If I don't run into Steven, and if Isabella doesn't call to remind me about the film at Theta house tonight, and if Elizabeth doesn't find out about the money I borrowed from her account until I have a chance to explain, then I'll never do anything to get myself into trouble again. Not ever.* She climbed out of the car, heaving her shopping bags after her. "This time I really mean it," she added out loud.

She glanced up at the window of her brother's apartment. She wouldn't put it past him to be peering from behind the curtains, waiting for her to come home so he could finish last night's argument, but the curtains remained closed and motionless.

And just one other thing, Jessica continued as she hurried into the building, *please don't let Mike be mad at me. Don't let him be mad at me and make him come home.*

112

She rested her groceries against the door while she searched through her bag for her keys. She put the key in the lock, and then she paused. It was too early for Mike to be home, but she thought she heard music coming from inside. It was an old crackling record of "Love Me Tender." It was their song. The one he'd played on their first date.

Slowly and silently, she turned the key in the lock. There were no lights on, but she thought she smelled something burning. She went inside. Yes, she did smell burning. Burning sweet-and-sour chicken. She moved toward the living room.

"Oh, my gosh," she breathed. The entire room was lit by candles: big candles, little candles, candles in holders, and candles in jars.

Mike stepped out of the shadows.

"What is this?" Jessica gasped.

He held out his arms. "I missed you last night, baby," Mike said. "I really did."

She walked into his embrace. "I missed you, too."

Billie picked up the telephone from the desk and banged it down on the coffee table in front of Steven. "There it is," she said. "All you have to do is pick up the receiver, dial your parents' number, and the whole thing will be out of your hands."

Steven stared at the telephone as though he expected it to explode. "I'm not sure that's the best way to handle this, Billie," he said calmly and thoughtfully.

After the scene with Jessica last night, Billie had accused him of being crazy and irrational. She'd said he behaved like a jealous lover, not a brother. She'd said he'd better get a grip on himself. So all day, he'd been practicing being sane and reasonable, and trying to get a grip on himself. He thought he was doing pretty well.

Billie, however, did not. "Oh, please," she said, sighing heavily. "Give me a break."

"Now what?" he demanded. "I thought you'd agree. You're the one who said Jessica's an adult now and has a right to her own life. You're the one who said I'm a hypocrite, living one way and expecting her to live another."

"And you're the one who's worrying himself sick," Billie said. She sat down across from him. "I've been thinking. Maybe the best thing would be to tell your parents. After all, they're the ones who support Jessica. They have a right to know what's going on. They should be the ones to decide what to do."

Steven shook his head. He'd been thinking about it, too. Sometimes it seemed to him that he thought of nothing else. Last night, while Billie slept peacefully beside him, he'd tossed and turned almost until dawn, trying to decide what really was the best course of action. Should he just ignore the whole thing and get on with his own life? Should he tell his parents?

But if he ignored what was going on, Jessica

could get into real trouble. Mike McAllery wasn't the kind to settle down or commit himself to one woman. Everyone knew that except Jessica. But the fact that the Corvette-driving creep would eventually break Jessica's heart seemed to Steven like the least of the problems. What if Jessica got pregnant? Or worse? What if McAllery gave her some disease?

On the other hand, if he told Mr. and Mrs. Wakefield, there was no doubt in Steven's mind what would happen. His father would pull Jessica out of Sweet Valley University and make her go somewhere closer to home where they knew where she was every night.

But Steven also knew his sister. She wasn't going to react well to that kind of tactics. If anything, it would probably push her even harder into Mike McAllery's arms. He could picture her dropping out of college and getting a job as a waitress so she could be with the man she loved.

"No," Steven said. "I've decided I have to take a course of action somewhere between doing nothing and doing too much."

Billie watched him, her expression politely curious.

"I've decided I have to break them up before it goes too far."

"Steven," Billie said. "They're living together. How much farther do you think it can go?"

Steven didn't answer. He wasn't even going to let the suggestion that his little sister might do something really stupid, like marry the Don Juan of Sweet Valley University, cross his lips.

"It can go a lot farther," he said. "She could get so involved that she couldn't get out even if she wanted to. Or he could dump her tomorrow and traumatize her for life."

Billie folded her hands on her lap. "May I ask just one little question?"

"Sure," Steven said, feeling better already now that a decision had been made. "What?"

"Just how are you planning to break them up?"

"I haven't quite worked that part out yet," he said.

Chapter Six

"Hey, I've got a great idea," Mike said.

Jessica paused to swallow a mouthful of cereal. "Another great idea?" she asked with a smile. "I don't think I can take more than one every few hours or so."

They were sitting on the couch together, wrapped in a blanket, watching cartoons and eating their breakfasts like little kids. That had been Mike's first great idea. Jessica couldn't remember a morning that had been this much fun.

He gave her a sugary kiss. "No, really," he said. "You're going to love this. It's the best one yet."

Jessica kissed a tiny dribble of milk from his chin. "All right," she said with a laugh. "What is it?"

"Come to work with me today."

Jessica turned to him in surprise. Making up last night had been wonderful, and having breakfast together like this was stupendous, but still she couldn't believe that he was actually asking her to spend the whole day with him.

Mike liked his space and his privacy, and a lot of his space and privacy existed in that place she'd never seen and he rarely talked about: that place called "work."

"Really?" she said. "Are you serious?"

He put his arm around her under the covers. "I want my baby with me as much as possible. You know that." He touched his lips to her hair. "I've never known anything like this before, Jess," he said, his voice barely audible over the television. "I've never had somebody care about me so much."

Jessica snuggled against him, her will melting away.

She was going to say that as much as she'd like to, she couldn't go to work with him. What about her classes? What about her other commitments? She wasn't going to mention that she still had to come up with some excuse for missing the Theta thing the night before, or that she had to get hold of her sister and explain about the loan Elizabeth had given her that she didn't know she'd given her, but these were things she absolutely had to do today.

But she couldn't do that. She didn't want him to think that she didn't care about him as much as he thought. Especially since she did; she cared more.

"I've never known anything like this before, either," Jessica whispered. "I didn't think a person could be this happy."

His lips moved down the side of her face. "Does that mean you'll come to my office with me?"

Jessica laughed. "I guess I should wear my old clothes for this, shouldn't I? I'm going to end up covered in grease."

"If you play your cards right," Mike said, "you could end up covered in kisses."

"He loves me," Celine said, pulling a petal from the rose in her hand and tossing it onto the floor. "He loves me not." Another petal joined the dozens already on the carpet. "He loves me . . . he loves me not . . ."

Through the window she watched Elizabeth and Nina Harper come out of Dickenson Hall and walk up the path, talking excitedly.

Celine knew what they were talking about; she'd overheard them whispering together when Nina came to get Elizabeth. They'd both thought Celine was still asleep.

"So the little worker bees have big dates," Celine said, yanking a few more petals loose and letting them drop. "How sweet."

From what Celine had overheard, Elizabeth was nervous about her date with William. He was so handsome and so intelligent, she'd said, but so mysterious as well. She didn't know what to expect from him.

Celine smiled, stroking a petal against her own soft, smooth cheek. "Expect the worst, sugar," she said as the two girls disappeared behind a building. "That's my advice."

Celine knew from experience that if you expected the worst, you were seldom disappointed. How many times had she let herself be fooled into thinking that this time her mother really was going to come home and spend some time with her? How many times had she convinced herself that her parents really were planning to take her to Paris with them instead of leaving her with granny in that dark old house?

Scary granny. Celine closed her eyes for a second. She could see the crumbling mansion and smell the jasmine in the garden and the gin and whiskey in Granny's room. She could hear the shouting and screaming: *Celine, Celine, you little witch! Celine, you come up here right this very second, you hear me? You come right now . . .*

Opening her eyes, Celine removed another rose from the vase. She pulled free a petal. "He loves me . . ." she murmured.

Did William White love Elizabeth Wakefield—was that what it was all about? Had the Prince of Darkness really lost his heart? Celine smiled into the sunny morning. People like William didn't fall in love with people like Elizabeth. People like

William didn't understand or want love. What they understood was power; what they wanted was control. And what Celine wanted was to see both William and Elizabeth destroyed.

She tossed one last petal onto the floor. "He loves me not."

Winston hurried out of his history class and started in the direction of the Sigma house. All the pledges were being given a special lunch today, as a reward for having come so far. An authentic English meal—fish and chips—one of the brothers had told him. Winston knew it wouldn't be a good idea to be late.

"Yo, Winston! Winston, wait up!"

Winston slowed down, hesitating. If it had been a sweet, friendly female voice calling him— the voice of Elizabeth or even Denise—Winston would have known what to do: keep right on walking. After his night with the goat, he wasn't taking any chances of incurring the anger of Peter Wilbourne III.

When the hazing started, Winston thought it was all just a joke, just fun. But he wasn't so sure anymore. It definitely wasn't the kind of fun he was used to. In fact, for the most part it was pure torture. But from now on he was going to do everything right. He wasn't going to stop to pet a cat unless the Sigma president said it was all right.

"Hey, Egbert! Slow down!"

But it wasn't a girl calling him, it was a guy. It might be Bill or Jeff or Tony, or one of his other big brothers. It might even be Peter Wilbourne III. If he ran away from Peter Wilbourne, he might as well not stop until he reached Mexico. Winston stopped. He turned around.

Oh no, Winston thought, *now I really am in trouble*. He looked nervously around to see if there were any Sigmas nearby. It was Elizabeth's friend, Tom Watts from WSVU. No one in the fraternity had liked Tom Watts since the night he made Peter Wilbourne look like a fool at the Sigma-Theta party, but now they officially loathed him. A lot of the Sigmas were jocks, or friends of jocks, and Tom's broadcast on the sports scandal had made him public enemy number one at Sigma. Winston had no doubt that if he could have, Peter Wilbourne would have put a price on Tom Watts's head.

Winston started to hurry again, but it was too late. Tom came jogging up beside him.

"Hi," Tom said. "Remember me? I met you with Elizabeth a few weeks ago. I—"

"I know who you are," Winston mumbled. He was getting pretty good at talking without moving his lips. "Go away."

He could feel Tom give him a quizzical look. "Come on, Winston. I just want to talk to you for a couple of minutes."

"I'm in a hurry," Winston hissed between clenched teeth. "Go away."

Tom didn't go away. He was in better shape than Winston—possibly because he had been a top athlete, possibly because he hadn't been walking around campus with a brick tied to his neck and sleeping on concrete with cloven-hooved animals. Tom easily kept the pace.

"It's about fraternity hazing," Tom said. "You know Elizabeth and I are doing a story about it. I thought that maybe you and I could go for a cup of coffee after class and have a little talk."

A little talk with Tom Watts, the Clark Kent of Sweet Valley University, Winston thought. *That's just what I need.*

"I can't help you," Winston said. "I already told Elizabeth. I've pledged to keep fraternity secrets, you know that."

"I'm not asking you to reveal the Sigma secrets," Tom said. "I just want to talk to you about your experiences. You know, get a firsthand picture."

"No," Winston growled. "I can't help—" He broke off as terror iced every cell of his body. Up ahead, getting into his maroon Jeep, was Peter Wilbourne. Winston was sure that Peter hadn't seen him, because if he had seen him, he'd probably be trying to run him down by now. "I gotta go," Winston said, starting to run. "I can't be late."

Winston was damp with sweat and breathless by the time he skidded into the Sigma dining room. Peter Wilbourne, of course, was already there, sitting at the head of the table.

He was smiling, something Winston was learning was not necessarily a good sign.

"Sit down, plebe Egbert," Peter said. "We were just about to start serving."

Winston sat down, beginning to relax as he saw the plates of french fries and battered cod being placed in front of the other plebes. Suddenly he was starving. He felt as though he hadn't eaten in days, which wasn't far from the truth. He watched a steaming dish appear in front of the plebe beside him. Winston's mouth began to water.

The brother who was acting as waiter stopped by Winston's shoulder. Winston looked down. The saliva dried in his mouth. Before him was a plate of wood chips. On the plate was a bowl of water containing five small goldfish.

"What's this?" Winston gasped.

Everyone else began to laugh.

"That," Peter Wilbourne said, laughing the loudest, "is the old English delicacy, fish and chips."

Elizabeth frowned as she checked the figure the bank teller had given her against the numbers in her checkbook. *This can't be right,* she thought, her eyes going from one to the other.

The computer must be on the blink or something.

According to Elizabeth's accounting, she should have had a hundred dollars more in the bank than the bank thought she had. *It's a good thing I always balance my checkbook or I might not have even noticed*. The image of her sister came to her mind. Jessica never wrote down how much she'd taken out or put in. She never read through her statements. "I let the bank take care of all that," Jessica always said. "That's its job."

Elizabeth looked up at the teller. She wasn't worried. Mistakes did happen, after all. The teller was watching her with a bored expression on his face.

"I'm sorry," Elizabeth said, "but there must be some mistake. Your balance doesn't match mine."

The teller shook his head. "There's no mistake," he said. "That's how much is left in your account."

"Couldn't you check it again?" she asked. "Computers make mistakes, too." She smiled politely.

The teller sighed. "If you really want me to get a printout for you, I will," he said. "But I'm sure this is correct. We went through it yesterday. Remember?"

"We?" Elizabeth stopped smiling. "What do you mean, we went through it yesterday?"

"You asked for a statement of your account, and then you withdrew a hundred dollars." He leaned forward. "I remember because I waited on you, and because I noticed your twin in here a little while before."

"My sister?" Elizabeth asked.

"Yeah, your sister." He winked. "I remember thinking that it's a good thing you two wear your hair differently or no one would ever be able to tell you apart."

Now she was definitely worried. No, she was more than worried, she was furious. Jessica had promised after impersonating her at the Homecoming game with Peter Wilbourne that she would never pull a stunt like that again, and here she was, only weeks later, taking money from Elizabeth's bank account. *Stealing!* Elizabeth fumed to herself. *Jessica stole my money!*

"You're right," Elizabeth said, scooping her things into her bag. "It's a good thing people can tell us apart."

Isabella was thinking of Jessica as she and Alison Quinn left the snack bar.

One of the reasons was that Isabella missed her. Their little apartment seemed empty and lonely without her. She'd gotten used to Jessica's endless energy and constant chattering. She'd looked forward to going home at the end of the day and having Jessica there to fix a meal with and discuss the day. Jessica made her laugh. Just sitting in the living room doing homework with her was fun— not that they ever got anything done.

And sometimes after they'd gone to bed and turned out the lights, they'd lie awake in the dark, talking about everything: from guys to the benefits of a cucumber facial to what they would do if someone gave them a million dollars.

Jessica was the only person Isabella had told about her crush on Tom Watts. The other day, when Tom helped her with the research for her sociology paper, she'd been so excited that she'd actually forgotten that Jessica wouldn't be there when she got back to the room. She was desperate to talk about him—how he'd looked, what he'd said, whether or not she should ask him out to the coffeehouse to thank him for his time— but of course when she got back to the dorm, she was all alone. She didn't have so much as a pet goldfish she could talk to. Even if she got a new roommate, Isabella knew that it wouldn't be the same.

The other reason Isabella was thinking about Jessica was that Alison was talking about her.

"I don't know what she thinks she's doing," Alison was saying in her perennially disapproving way, "but she'd better stop pretty quickly if she wants to become a full-fledged Theta."

"I told you what happened last night," Isabella said. "She had really bad cramps. She could barely move." Isabella had promised herself that she wasn't going to cover for Jessica, but somehow she found herself doing it. "And besides, Alison, you know what it's like when you're a freshman—everything's so new and different, and there's so much to do . . . It can be a little overwhelming."

Alison gave her a look. "I know classes are important," she said evenly. "But the sorority is important, too. She's not going to get very far on this campus if she's dropped by Theta Alpha Theta." Alison made a sound that from anyone less attractive and sophisticated would have been a snort. "Between you and me, Izzy, since Elizabeth Wakefield resigned her pledge, neither Magda nor I see much point in keeping Jessica on if she doesn't show more loyalty and group spirit." She made that sound again. "She's missed two nights already."

They walked out of the building and into the quad.

"She didn't feel well," Isabella said, trying not to sound weary. "You can't punish her for not feeling well."

Alison seemed to be thinking this over for a few seconds. Suddenly she gave Isabella a poke in the arm. "My God, will you look who's coming?" she said in a voice sort of like a stage whisper. "What a relief that she dropped out of Theta. She looks more and more bohemian every day."

Isabella bit back a smile. Elizabeth Wakefield might not be wearing a tailored suit, as Alison was, or have spent two hours that morning curling her hair and plucking her eyebrows, but Isabella wouldn't have called her bohemian. She was wearing faded Levi's, an almost antique-looking floral-patterned vest, Doc Martens on her feet, and silver bangles around one wrist. She was striking, unique. And Isabella thought she looked beautiful.

Much to Isabella's surprise, instead of sailing past them, Elizabeth stopped in front of her. "Have you seen Jessica?" she demanded. "Is she in a class or is she back at your room?"

What's Jessica done now? Isabella wondered, noticing the flush in Elizabeth's cheeks and the anger in her eyes.

"Class," Isabella said immediately. "She has a couple of classes this afternoon."

"Well, tell her I'll be over later," Elizabeth said grimly. "Tell her to stick around. I really need to talk to her."

That's great. Just what I need, Elizabeth coming over and finding out that Jessica doesn't live there anymore.

"Oh, gee," Isabella said, aware that Alison was watching her closely. "I'm not sure she's coming back after school. I think she has something to do tonight. Why don't I ask her to give you a call?"

"I'm glad to hear that Jessica's recovered so quickly," Alison said.

*   *   *

129

Tom leaned back in his chair, his eyes on the screen, his expression thoughtful. He'd put all the data Elizabeth had gathered on the computer, using the graphics software to make charts and graphs. The result was virtually a picture. The only trouble was, he wasn't quite sure what the picture was of.

"Okay," Tom said, "so we know for sure that *something's* going on."

"Go back," Elizabeth said. Her shoulder brushed his as she moved toward the screen. "Go back to the chart of the 'accidental' deaths."

"We've already looked at it backwards and forwards and upside down," Tom said. "I don't know what else we can get from it." Nonetheless, he hit the Page Up key several times, moving back to the page Elizabeth wanted. "Drownings, road accidents, a heart attack, two electrocutions—one in which a radio fell in the bath and the other one from faulty wiring . . . The only pattern in the deaths themselves is that they really could have been accidents."

Elizabeth nodded in agreement. "Except that they all happened during hazing, and except that there's one every seven years without fail from the fifties on." She tapped her pencil on the edge of his desk. "Every seven years . . ."

"And except that every death was of a Sigma pledge," Tom added. He gave a grim laugh. "They should make it part of their motto:

Sigma—Fraternity, Loyalty, Murder."

"Maybe I should try talking to Winston again," Elizabeth suggested.

Tom shook his head. "Forget it, Elizabeth. I tried myself, but he's so scared, the only thing he'll say is 'go away.'"

Elizabeth chewed on her bottom lip, studying the chart. "I don't know, Tom," she said slowly. "I just feel like we're missing something. Some link."

"What kind of link?"

She laughed in mock-exasperation. "If I knew that, Dr. Watts, we wouldn't be sitting here staring at the computer like two couch potatoes, would we? We'd be out there with our bloodhounds, tracking down the culprits."

"All right, all right." Tom laughed too, but he was still deep in thought. "Seven years," he repeated. "You think there's something in that, Elizabeth? The fact that it's seven years and not five or twelve or four?"

She nodded. "I think maybe there is. After all, seven is one of those special numbers, isn't it? It's always been used in rituals and magic and—"

"Secret societies," Tom finished.

She looked at him, thinking it over. "That's right," she said. He could see her brain working as understanding began to show in her eyes. "Secret societies."

Tom felt a rush of excitement. "I think we may have found that missing link," he said, grabbing her arm. "The famous secret society. Maybe that's what separates Sigma from the other fraternities."

Elizabeth put her hand on his shoulder, leaning her head so close to his that their foreheads almost touched. "Slow down," she ordered. "We may have identified the missing link, but we haven't actually found it yet. I'll go back to the library and look through those papers again. Only, this time I'll look for what else was going on at the same time. You never know, the clue might be in the most innocent little story."

Tom felt like hugging her. He felt like jumping up and dancing her around the room. "You're brilliant, you know that?" Tom grinned. "How did I ever accomplish anything here before you came along?"

Elizabeth glowed at his praise. "I've told you before," she said, blushing. "I've had a great teacher."

Overcome with his feelings for her, Tom didn't think about what he was going to say next for a change. He just let his thoughts come out as words. "Hey, I've got an idea," he said. "Why don't we go through the newspapers together, and then later we can go for a pizza or something."

For a second, he thought she was going to say yes. He was sure she was. He could see it in her eyes.

But she didn't. She said no.

"Oh, gee, Tom," she said. "I'd lo—I'd really like that, but I'm . . . um . . . see, I already have plans for tonight."

He pulled back from her. "Sure," he said. "I understand. I should've known you'd be busy."

He should have known she'd say no. Who was he kidding? Who was she kidding? If she had any interest in him, she would have mentioned the poem days ago; she must know it was from him.

That's what you get, Tom told himself. *You put your heart out where someone can see it and they either step on it or walk right by.*

"Maybe another time . . ." Elizabeth murmured.

"Yeah, sure," Tom said. "Maybe another time."

While she got ready for her date with William, Elizabeth was thinking about Tom. She'd felt so close to him when they were working on the hazing story, sitting there beside him, feeling his excitement and knowing it was just like her own. If she closed her eyes, she could still see his face when he told her that he didn't know what he'd done without her. She was sure there had been something more than professional admiration in his face and his voice.

She pulled a long, black silk dress from her closet. It would have seemed a little too formal for a date with an ordinary guy, but William White was anything but ordinary. Black silk seemed perfect for dinner with him. Especially since, because

133

of its cut, it was the only dress she had that wasn't still too tight.

"I can't believe Tom didn't write that poem," Elizabeth mumbled to herself as she slipped into the dress. So much for the power of positive thinking. She'd wanted it to be Tom so badly that she'd convinced herself of it.

Elizabeth gave herself a wry look in the mirror. She was still convincing herself. Even though she knew William was the author, she was still somehow hoping it was Tom. It didn't *sound* like William, or *feel* like William. She recalled Tom's face when he asked her to dinner. She'd felt like shouting at him then, *Why didn't you ask me sooner? Why didn't you send me that poem?*

Elizabeth twisted her hair into a knot on top of her head and held it in place with some large black clips. If she were going out with Tom and not William, she'd be putting on something casual right now. They'd probably go for pizza or to the taqueria in town. If she were going out with Tom, she'd be looking forward to the night ahead. As it was, she had no idea what to expect.

Elizabeth leaned closer to the mirror to put on her silver earrings. If she were going out with Tom, she would have expected perfection.

"I didn't even know you had a car," Elizabeth said as she slid into the passenger side of the silver convertible Karmann Ghia. The antique car was flawlessly restored. She'd been in some very nice and very expensive cars in the past, but nothing quite like this. Like everything else about William White, it was so elegant and stylish it hardly seemed real.

William shut the door and came around to the other side, getting in behind the wheel. "There's a lot you don't know about me," he said, looking over at her. He smiled. "And there's a lot I don't know about you." From under his seat he produced a small, clear plastic box. Inside was a corsage of miniature white roses. "But I'm going to try to find out."

It almost sounded like a threat. *Don't be ridiculous,* Elizabeth scolded herself. *He's not threatening you, he's flirting with you.* Maybe she should have gotten back into the dating scene sooner. She was more out of practice than she'd imagined.

"I thought I was the investigative reporter," she kidded.

He handed her the box of flowers. "Just assure me that you're not on duty now," William answered. His smile was bright and charming. "I don't like anyone prying into my affairs."

As she smiled back into that pale, fine face and those eyes that gave nothing away, she felt a chill run through her. What was wrong with her? Why couldn't she tell the difference between a threat and a joke anymore?

William reached over and took the lid from the box, lifting out the corsage. "Hey, don't look so serious. I was only teasing." His long, thin fingers fastened the roses to her dress. "I want us to have a perfect evening," he said, his voice as soft and gentle as the evening breeze. "The first of many."

"Here," Denise said, kneeling beside Winston. "Drink some ginger ale. When I was a little kid, my mother always gave me ginger ale when I was sick."

Winston groaned. He was sitting on the floor, propped against the wall. One of the problems with dorm life was that you couldn't even throw up in private. The bathroom had been empty when he'd first staggered in there, so ill from his lunch of wood chips and goldfish, he thought he was going to die and didn't care. The minute he started to be sick, though, Anoushka and Debbie had appeared out of nowhere, and now half the floor was hovering around him, offering advice and sympathy.

"Come on," Denise urged. "It really works."

Not when you've eaten wood and live fish, it doesn't, Winston thought. How could he have been so stupid? Was this really the way he wanted to spend the next four years of his life, hanging out with a bunch of guys who thought making you sleep with goats and eat goldfish was funny?

Winston had this terrible worry prickling the back of his mind. He couldn't help wondering if the only reason the Sigmas had pledged him was to make him the butt of their jokes. After all, he wasn't exactly Sigma material, was he? He wasn't rich, his parents weren't famous, he wasn't a jock. The other frat brothers were all destined for big jobs in politics or business, but he was just a regular guy. A new wave of nausea rose in his throat.

"I don't need ginger ale," he gasped. "I need strychnine. It's the only thing that will make me feel better."

Maia came up on his other side, pressing a cold cloth to his head. "Why don't you go lie down, Winnie?" she asked. "I've emptied out your trash basket and put it by your bed. You know, in case you're sick again."

Denise took him tenderly by his left arm. "Come on. We'll help you to your room," she said. She shook her head, watching the color drain from Winston's face as he got to his feet. "I really hope you've learned your lesson, Winnie. I hope the next time those bozos want you to do something dumb like this, you'll say no."

Elizabeth giggled as she let herself into her pitch-dark dorm room. This was the first time since the term began that she hadn't been in bed before Celine. She bumped into the closet and giggled some more. It was also the first time that she'd come back a little tipsy.

That's okay, Elizabeth told herself as she kicked

137

off her shoes. *What's good enough for the Southern Belle is good enough for the California Princess.*

Elizabeth hadn't really intended to drink any of the wine that was ordered with dinner. The casually charming William White, however, was as comfortable in a sophisticated, glamorous restaurant as other men his age were in a pizza parlor. He was so effortlessly at home with wine lists and exotic menus that Elizabeth soon found herself following his lead. He recommended a salad and main course, and Elizabeth had them. They were delicious. He filled her glass with the white Californian wine and she drank it. That was delicious, too.

Halfway through the meal, she'd caught their reflection in the mirror on the wall. They'd looked like a couple in a film or a magazine. Young, blond, and beautiful.

There they were in Da Vinci's, the most expensive and elegant restaurant in the area, ordering grilled shrimp with lime and cilantro and dry white wine, and she'd thought, *Why not?* She was a college woman now. She was with a man who was so interesting and charming he might have walked out of a nineteenth-century novel. What was wrong with one little glass of wine?

Elizabeth stepped out of her dress, lost her balance, and landed in her chair in a new wave of giggles. In the end, it had been a perfect evening. Everything William said was either funny or interesting. Everything he did was perfect. Every compliment he paid her made her feel as if she really was as wonderful as he seemed to think. It had been a long time since a man had made her feel this good about herself.

"If you're done crashing around like a drunken ox," said a grumpy voice from the other bed, "maybe you'll let me get some sleep."

Chapter Seven

Jessica looked around the familiar kitchen. Sometimes she felt as though she'd always lived with Mike. It was hard to believe that there'd been a time when his toothbrush wasn't next to hers in the bathroom and when there weren't his favorite things, apricot nectar and blueberry yogurt, always in the refrigerator. It was even harder for her to believe that there'd been a time when she didn't fall asleep with his arm around her and his "Good night, baby" whispered in her ear.

But at this moment, she was almost able to forget that she'd ever met Mike at all. There was Isabella, making them coffee and heating up croissants just as she used to. Jessica's name tag from her first Theta tea was still on the bulletin board above her old desk, along with the SVU pennant she'd bought at the Homecoming game, and several of the postcards from Lila in Italy.

"Oh, look," Jessica said to Isabella's back. "You still have that picture of us from Halloween night on the door of the fridge."

"Of course I do," Isabella said. "Officially, you still live here, remember?"

Jessica sighed as she watched Isabella pour two cups of cappuccino from her coffee machine. "It's just like old times, isn't it?" she asked brightly. "You and me having breakfast together . . . It really feels like I still live here."

Isabella handed her a cup. "Not exactly," she said, picking up the plate of croissants and leaving the room.

Jessica frowned as she followed her friend to the table. There was something in Isabella's voice that suggested that she hadn't invited Jessica over for coffee just for old times' sake. And Jessica hadn't accepted the invitation just for old times' sake, either.

"Well, of course it isn't exactly," Jessica said with a laugh. She sat down in her old place. "After all, I don't live here, do I?" She took a tentative sip of the steaming liquid in the pale blue cup. "But it is nice to be here again." Her smile became almost shy. "I do miss you, Izz."

Isabella passed her the plate of soft, crumbly rolls. "You can't miss me half as much as I miss you," she said.

Once again Jessica frowned. Despite her words, Isabella didn't sound particularly affectionate; she sounded annoyed.

"But you're not the one who has to act as though you really do live here, are you?" Isabella asked. "I'm the one who has to remember to say 'Jessica and I did this last night . . .' and 'Jessica's away for the weekend.'"

Jessica groaned inwardly. This wasn't what she'd wanted to hear from Isabella. This was not the best time for Isabella to be getting into a bad mood.

What about the week Jessica was having? The Thetas were unhappy with her, she'd missed an entire day of classes yesterday, she was in trouble with the bank, if she didn't talk to Elizabeth soon she was going to be in trouble with her twin, and if she couldn't get hold of some money she was either going to starve to death or have to go to her parents on bended knees.

"I have my problems, too, you know," Jessica cut in. "I've got Steven on my case. He watches me like the secret police or something. Do you think it's easy living with that?"

"Do you think it's easy covering for you all the time?" Isabella countered. "Yesterday I had to lie for you to Alison Quinn *and* to Elizabeth." She pushed away her plate, folding her hands in front of her. "There are just so many excuses I can make for you, Jess. People are beginning to wonder why you're never here when they drop by. It was all I could do to stop your sister from coming here looking for you yesterday."

"I know, I know." Jessica brushed Isabella's

143

words away with her hand. Besides inviting her to breakfast, Isabella had called her in a small panic last night to tell her that her twin was looking for her. "I told you I called her. I'm seeing Elizabeth for lunch."

"That's fine, Jess," Isabella said. "But it's not enough." She leaned forward, her expression earnest. "How long do you really think you can keep this up? Because I'm telling you right now, I can't keep it up much longer. Alison Quinn will strangle me with my own panty hose when she finds out I've been conspiring with you."

Jessica looked straight into Isabella's eyes. She wasn't quite sure what to say next. The real reason Jessica had jumped at the invitation for this morning, even though it meant not having breakfast with Mike, was that she was hoping to borrow enough money from Isabella to hold her until Thanksgiving. She was sure that by the time she went home for Thanksgiving, she would have come up with some good excuse to give her parents for being overdrawn, but she needed time.

"Well, to tell you the truth, Izz," Jessica began slowly, "that's kind of what I wanted to talk to you about."

"Really?" A look of relief came over Isabella's lovely face. "You mean, you're coming back to the dorm?"

"Coming back to the dorm?" Jessica screeched. She was a good actress, but even she couldn't pretend that the idea of leaving Mike didn't horrify her. "Isabella, I can't come back to the dorm. What about Mike?"

"Oh, Mike . . . Right." Isabella rolled her eyes. "I just thought you meant you'd reconsidered the situation and realized how impossible it is."

Jessica nodded, carefully choosing her words. "It is impossible at the moment, but it's not because of having to lie to the Thetas and Elizabeth."

Isabella's large eyes narrowed suspiciously. "It isn't?"

Jessica shook her head, the golden hair swirling around her shoulders. "No, it isn't." She made her own face serious and mature. "It's because I'm having a little cash flow problem at the moment."

"Cash flow problem?" Isabella echoed. She leaned even closer. "Jessica, I'm talking about trying to live two lives when most people have enough trouble living one. What does that have to do with your cash flow problem?"

Jessica chewed nervously on her bottom lip. There was no way out; she was going to have to tell Isabella the truth. "I won't be living one life if I don't get some money from somewhere," she said in a rush. As briefly as she could—and leaving out the part where she pretended to be Elizabeth— Jessica explained what had happened at the bank. "So you see," she finished, "I really need a loan until I can get my parents to give me some more money."

145

Isabella was staring at her with a look Jessica recognized. She had seen it so many times before on so many different people—and always in reaction to one of her schemes. It was amazement. Dumbstruck, one hundred percent, unconditional amazement.

"Are you saying you want *me* to lend you money?" Isabella asked when she finally found her voice. "Is that what you're saying, Jess? That besides covering for you and turning myself inside out to keep your secret, you want me to lend you money?"

"It would only be for a little while, Isabella," Jessica promised quickly. "Maybe a month. Two at the most."

Isabella shook her head. "No," she said simply. "I'm not going to bail you out of this one. You made your bed, now you have to lie in it."

Jessica hid her face behind her coffee cup so Isabella couldn't see how disappointed she was.

Well, at least my bed is with Mike, she consoled herself.

Elizabeth looked up as her sister came out of the cafeteria line with a loaded tray.

Jessica was wearing a long, filmy pink dress half-buttoned down the front, and under it a charcoal gray bodysuit. She had a pink silk scarf around her hair. The effect was so stunning that Elizabeth wasn't the only one watching Jessica

146

come into the lunchroom. There was hardly a male in the place who wasn't staring in Jessica's direction, his lunch forgotten.

That's my sister, Elizabeth thought with a wry smile. *Even if the whole cafeteria were packed with models, she'd still make an entrance.*

Seeing her twin across the room, Jessica smiled and waved. Elizabeth stopped herself from smiling and waving back. *Remember that you're mad at her,* she chided herself. *Remember why you're here.*

If Jessica noticed that her sister wasn't overjoyed to see her, she gave no indication as she put her tray down and threw herself into the chair across from Elizabeth.

"It's amazing what stress and anxiety can do to you," Jessica said, in her usual breathless rush of words. "I am starving, Elizabeth, absolutely starving." She shook her head. "I'm telling you, you wouldn't want the week I've had for anything. It's like the whole universe is on my case."

"Is that so?" Elizabeth asked, watching her sister bite into an oversized club sandwich as though she hadn't eaten in days.

"Uh-huh," Jessica said, made silent for a moment by the necessity to chew. Finally she looked at Elizabeth. "What do you call that?" she asked, pointing in horror at the tray in front of her twin.

Elizabeth looked at the small undressed salad, dry rye crackers, apple, and glass of water on her tray. Her diet had reached another of its many plateaus. She'd lose a pound or two and be feeling really positive about always being hungry, and then all of a sudden she wouldn't lose an ounce even after starving herself for days on end.

"Lunch," Elizabeth said.

"Lunch?" Jessica wiped at her mouth with a napkin. "Lunch for what? A rabbit?" Jessica stuffed a french fry into her mouth. "Are you on some kind of diet?" She stopped eating for a second, looking Elizabeth up and down. "You don't look that fat," she said, as though this should comfort her sister.

"Thanks," Elizabeth mumbled. "I'm glad you think so."

Jessica shrugged. "Of course, it's hard to tell, the way you're dressing lately." She grabbed another french fry. "What you need to do is start dating, Elizabeth. You know, get back into the swing of things."

Elizabeth had resolved to keep the conversation on money and sisters who took money that wasn't theirs without asking, but she couldn't resist mentioning what she'd done the night before. "As a matter of fact—" she began.

Jessica talked right over her. "And you should have stuck with the Thetas," she went on. "It would give you something to do besides homework."

"I have a lot of things to do besides homework," Elizabeth said.

Jessica didn't hear that either. "I've been so busy

with the sorority—you know, parties and socials and film nights and stuff like that . . ." She laughed, her sea-green eyes sparkling. "That's why you haven't seen me much," she said. "I'm just *so* busy."

Elizabeth had taken up her fork, but she dropped it. "You mean busy spending my money," she said.

The bright, bubbly smile on Jessica's face flickered. "You know?"

"Yes," Elizabeth said. "I know."

Jessica nodded. "Well, that's why I wanted to talk to you," she said, as though meeting for lunch had been her idea. "I was going to tell you right away—yesterday—but things got so hectic—"

"Jessica, how could you do that?" Elizabeth finally exploded. "You've done some pretty awful things in your life, but to pretend you were me and steal money from my account . . ."

"*Steal?*" Jessica looked thunderstruck at this accusation. "Elizabeth, you know I would never *steal* from you. I just borrowed it, that's all. Temporarily. I'm going to pay you back as soon as I can."

"Borrowed it? Without telling me?"

"But I couldn't tell you, Elizabeth. You weren't there."

It always amazed Elizabeth just how sincere and passionate Jessica became when she was caught doing something wrong.

"It was an emergency," she added.

"What kind of emergency?" Elizabeth asked.

Jessica made a typical exasperated-Jessica face.

"The kind of emergency where you only have fifty-five cents in your account, that's what kind."

Elizabeth laughed. "Fifty-five cents? Oh, come on, Jess, you're going to have to do better than that."

"But it's true!" Jessica squealed. "That's how much I have left."

Elizabeth watched her, searching for a sign that she was kidding. "You can't. You and I started out with the exact same amount at the beginning of the semester. I know you're extravagant, but you couldn't have spent all that money already."

"Wanna bet?" Jessica bit into her pickle. "Maybe you were right, never going out or dressing up or doing anything," she said grudgingly. "At least it's cheap."

"So now what?" Elizabeth asked. She picked up her fork again. "When are you going to give me back my hundred dollars, and how are you planning to live for the rest of the semester on fifty-five cents?"

Jessica's eyes suddenly looked incredibly blue and incredibly large, as though she were a small, vulnerable, and trusting child. "Well, to tell you the truth, Elizabeth . . ."

Elizabeth was already shaking her head. "Oh no, you don't. You're not getting another cent from me, Jessica. And if you don't work out some way of paying me back, I'm going to tell Mom and Dad."

"What?" Jessica looked at Elizabeth in horror. "Elizabeth, you wouldn't do that."

Elizabeth nodded. She knew her sister well enough to know that Jessica thought she could get away with anything. This time, Elizabeth had decided, Jessica was going to have to accept the responsibility for what she'd done.

"You're the one who's always talking about how grown up we are now that we're college women," Elizabeth said. "I think it's about time you started acting like it."

Jessica stared at her for several seconds in silence. She leaned back in her chair. "You're right, Elizabeth," she said at last. "It is about time I started acting like a responsible adult." She smiled triumphantly. "I know exactly what I'm going to do," she said. "I'm going to get a job."

Elizabeth almost choked on her cracker. "You are?"

Jessica? Get a job? Anyone who knew Jessica knew that she and work had never been compatible.

"And I thought it was amazing that I finally went on a date!" Elizabeth said, starting to laugh.

After lunch, refusing to admit how hungry she still was, Elizabeth went back to the library to continue her research for the WSVU piece, but her mind was on her sister.

You have to hand it to Jess, she was thinking as she strolled across the campus. *She may be infuriating, but she really is something.* Who else could "borrow" a hundred dollars from you without asking and still make you laugh so much you were almost in tears?

Elizabeth smiled to herself as she remembered some of Jessica's stories about the ridiculous games the Thetas played on their pledges. Most of their pranks concerned forcing pledges to confess deep dark secrets like how much they spent on clothes or whether they would ever go out with a run in their stocking.

Hefting her books in her arms, Elizabeth turned left, toward the large brick library building. Only one thing puzzled her about her lunch with Jessica. The name Mike McAllery didn't come up once. Normally if Jessica was dating someone, she couldn't shut up about him. Every other sentence would be, "Mike said this . . ." or "Mike thinks that . . ." But Elizabeth had eaten her salad, her crackers, and her apple—and Jessica had eaten enough for two marathon runners—without mentioning him once. Could it be that the romance was over already? Elizabeth wondered as she climbed the library steps.

Maybe she came to her senses, Elizabeth told herself with some relief. After all, Jessica had decided to get a job to pay Elizabeth back. Maybe that meant she really was growing up, that she'd finally realized how wrong Michael McAllery was for her.

"Elizabeth! Elizabeth! Wait up!"

Elizabeth turned at the top of the stairs. Racing

after her was Denise Waters. Elizabeth smiled and waved. Denise was one of the few Thetas she had actually gotten along with. Elizabeth had only gone out for Theta Alpha Theta because her mother had belonged when she was at college and because Jessica had her heart set on joining. But except for Denise, Elizabeth had found the girls almost laughably shallow.

"I'm so glad to see you," Denise said as she reached the library door. "I've been wanting to talk to you, but you know what it's like . . . One minute it's Monday and the next minute it's Friday."

Elizabeth laughed. "I know what you mean."

Denise's expression became serious. "Actually, I wanted to talk to you about Winston," she said, steering Elizabeth over to one side.

Instinctively, Elizabeth lowered her voice. "What's wrong?" she asked.

Denise glanced around. "I'm really worried about him," she said.

Elizabeth found herself checking who was nearby, too. "You mean because of the Sigma hazing?" she asked, almost whispering.

Denise nodded. "Yesterday they made him eat wood chips and live goldfish."

"What?" Elizabeth made a face. "You're kidding."

Denise shook her head. "That's just the beginning. You should've seen how sick he was."

"I've been trying to talk to him," Elizabeth

said, "but he won't even speak to me on the phone."

"I know," Denise said. "It's because you wanted to interview him for the TV station. I think he's really afraid, Elizabeth. I mean *really*. Not just this we-fraternity-brothers-have-secrets-no-mere-mortal-is-allowed-to-know-about stuff. I've seen dozens of guys go through fraternity hazings, but it was nothing like this. This is completely different."

"What can I do?" Elizabeth asked, feeling chilled by the somberness of Denise's expression.

"I don't think there's anything you can do," Denise said. "I mean, you're writing your story for WSVU. I just wanted you to know that if there's anything I or the other women in the dorm can do to help you, just ask."

Elizabeth was still standing on the library steps after she'd said good-bye to Denise, staring out across the quad. A dark, cold thought was creeping into her mind. A thought about Winston and the seven-year cycle of fraternity deaths. "Let's hope I don't need your help," she whispered.

It was an omen. An omen that her life was going in exactly the direction it was supposed to be going. She really had been destined to meet Mike, fall in love, and live with him. Jessica knew this beyond any doubt because just when things seemed bleakest—just when it looked as though she really might have to move back into the dorm with Isabella to keep her parents from finding out about her money situation—there, in the window of the coffeehouse, was a HELP WANTED sign.

"My lucky day!" Jessica cried, snatching the piece of cardboard as she sailed through the door.

Head up, she marched straight to the door marked OFFICE and knocked three times.

"Come in!" called a weary voice.

Jessica opened the door. The coffeehouse office was small and windowless. The walls, like the walls of the restaurant itself, were covered with newspaper and magazine clippings and concert posters. There was a desk in one corner, piled high with papers, and sitting at the desk was a small, dark, middle-aged man.

"What do you want?" he asked sourly as Jessica stepped into the room.

"I'm the answer to your prayers," she said, giving him one of her best smiles. She held up the sign. "I'm your new waitperson."

The man looked her up and down. *"You?"* he spluttered. "You want to *work?"*

Of course I don't want *to work!* Jessica felt like shouting at him. *Nobody in their right mind wants to* work, *but I don't really have much choice.* Instead, she stepped up her smile. "Yes, *me.* I need a job and I have experience."

"As a waitress?" the manager asked sarcastically.

Jessica tossed her head. "Yes," she said, "as a

155

waitress." Which was technically true. She had once been a waitress for four consecutive hours. Unfortunately, just as she was getting the hang of the job, some of her friends had stopped by for food on their way to the beach, and she'd handed back her apron and gone with them.

The manager raised his eyes to the ceiling. "Some answer to my prayers," he said. "I need a waitress who can carry twelve tables and work till she drops, and what do I get? A sorority girl."

"I am not," Jessica snapped. If she didn't need the job so desperately, she would have ripped up his sign and thrown it at him. "I am a mature, intelligent college woman who has been eating steadily for eighteen years and knows her way around food."

The manager was still eyeing her skeptically. "But you are in a sorority, aren't you?" he asked at last. "Haven't I seen you in here with your friends?"

Jessica's smile was sweeter than taffy. "Are you saying that you won't hire sorority members?" she asked. "Are you saying that you discriminate against us?"

He shook his head. "I'm not saying that. I'm just saying that I've never known one of you sorority types willing to bust her butt for minimum wage."

"Because if that is what you're saying," Jessica continued, ignoring him completely, "then I'm going to have to organize the biggest boycott this campus has ever seen." If her smile were any sweeter, it would have stuck to her teeth. "And I can do it," she promised. "There won't be a fraternity or sorority on campus who will come here after I'm through."

He pretended to shudder. "Gee, I'm scared."

"Well, you should be," Jessica said, inspired by her anger. "It just so happens that my sister works for WSVU. This is just the kind of story she loves."

His expression didn't change for a few seconds, and then he made a resigned face and held out his hand for the sign. "Welcome to *Lifestyles of the Rich and Famous,*" he said. "I'm Artie Stigman, but you can call me sir."

Jessica held out her hand. "And you can call me Ms. Wakefield."

If Celine Boudreaux looked like anything as she floated through the night in a cloud of silk and perfume, it was an angel. A tall, slender angel, a forest green velvet cape flowing behind her shoulders instead of wings.

Celine Boudreaux, however, didn't feel like an angel. Unless it was an avenging angel. The night was warm and the sky was bright with moonlight and stars, but Celine's thoughts were dark and slightly murderous as she trampled over the grass, her high heels making deep holes in the soft earth.

Last night, for a change, it was Celine who lay awake till after midnight, waiting for her roommate to come home. Smoking one cigarette after another, she stared at the ceiling, imagining how Elizabeth's date with William was going. Every five or six minutes she checked the time.

She imagined the date going well. William would buy Elizabeth more flowers, take her to the best restaurant, order the most exquisite meal and most delectable wine. He would compliment her, listen to her, encourage her, dazzle her with his knowledge and wit. No one knew better than Celine exactly how charming William White could be when he wanted. After all, the White family hadn't built its vast business empire by acting like barbarians. Barbarians screamed and drooled when they were knifing you, but the Whites just smiled and said something witty.

She imagined the date going badly. Elizabeth would bore William, just as the mouse eventually bores the cat. She would talk about journalism and her principles and how important it was to work hard. Elizabeth would tell him how she hated smoking, drinking, partying, and just plain having fun. She would numb him with goodness. By the time dessert came, William would be sound asleep.

It wasn't until Celine heard the shuffling and whispering outside her door, however, that she realized the date had gone better than she'd expected.

Celine kicked a small stone out of her way as she strode on. She hadn't expected to be lying there like her own old granny, listening to the sound of a good-night kiss on the other side of the door. That she had not expected.

"Yuck, imagine kissing Little Miss Perfect," Celine muttered as she turned up the path to the Sigma party. "She probably made him brush his teeth first."

She stopped at the front door. Inside she could hear loud voices and music. Colored lights shone through the windows of the fraternity house. Just for a second, she didn't hear or see any of it. She heard the deep, sensuous voice of William White whispering good night. She heard the sound of a tentative and tender kiss. She imagined those lips pressed to hers, those arms around her, that voice whispering something sweet and gentle in her ear.

"Well, look who's here," said another deep voice, but not the one she'd been thinking of. "I've been waiting for you."

Celine opened her eyes. Standing in front of her, one arm stretched across the door frame, was Peter Wilbourne III. He was smiling at her in the way she'd always wanted William White to smile at her.

But Peter Wilbourne, of course, was not William White. Peter Wilbourne was a murky gray sea slug next to William. Peter was a barbarian. He was cruel and nasty, two qualities Celine found irresistible, but compared to William he was common and crude. About the only advantage he had was that he was there.

"And here I am," Celine said, giving him a long, slow look. She smiled as she ducked under his arm and brushed past him. He was already a little drunk.

"I hope I'm the reason you came tonight," he said as he followed her unsteadily into the room, where she discarded her cape.

Celine turned, putting one hand gently against his chest. She did it to keep him from falling on top of her, but she knew he would think it was an affectionate gesture.

"What other reason could there be?" she purred.

Chapter Eight

Tom had lost count. He slowly lowered the barbells to the floor, his chest heaving rhythmically, trying to remember whether he was on seventy-five when he stopped counting or eighty-five.

He stared at the ceiling. It was useless. He might have been on two hundred and five for all he knew. All he could think of was that the stain on the ceiling looked a little like a rose.

"Damn Celine Boudreaux," Tom muttered, sitting up and wiping the sweat from his forehead with his T-shirt. "I hope her hair falls out."

The night before, Tom had had another strange encounter with Celine. He'd been working at the studio most of the night, going over the new material Elizabeth had given him, and Celine had been coming back from a party. She was weaving across the lawn, carrying her shoes and singing "Dixie" off-key. As much as he disliked Celine,

Tom couldn't let her go back to her dorm in that condition by herself.

"Chump," Tom said now, getting to his feet. "You should've left her alone. Maybe she'd be back in Louisiana by now, annoying the swamp gators."

As soon as Celine recognized him, the first words out of her mouth had been, "Isn't it too wonderful about Elizabeth and William White?"

Tom had tried to ignore her, but she wouldn't let him. Every time he tried to talk about something else—the weather, the food in the cafeteria, the political situation in South America—Celine kept right on babbling about Elizabeth and William and how romantic it was. She was still talking when they reached the entrance to the dorm.

"They do make such a stunning couple, don't you think?" she drawled. "They're both so *blond* and *beautiful* . . ."

Not really meaning to, he'd opened the door and practically thrown her inside.

Tom picked up the weights and put them back in his closet a lot more gently than he'd shoved Celine through the doors of Dickenson Hall.

So he'd been right. Elizabeth wasn't interested in him; she was interested in Mr. Mystery. What a fool he was.

Tom picked up his towel and shaving equipment. *It doesn't matter,* he told himself as he left his room. It's not like I have a big crush on her or anything. *It's really always been a professional relationship. And that's the way it'll stay.*

"What a beautiful day!" Celine cried, tearing back the curtains and sitting on her bed with a big smile. A halfhearted drizzle was falling over the campus from a dreary gray sky.

Elizabeth, brushing her hair in front of her dresser, looked over warily. "Has someone given you a personality transplant or something?" she asked. "You're not usually in this good a mood in the morning."

Celine reached for her cigarettes. The Little Princess was right, of course. Morning was not really Celine's favorite time of day. It ran in the family. All of the Boudreaux preferred the hours between sunset and dawn. But this morning she was feeling good. Really good. Not only had she had a very rewarding conversation with Tom Watts last night on her way back to the dorm, but she'd had a better time with Peter Wilbourne than she would have thought possible—considering that he wasn't William White.

"It was a great party," Celine said.

Elizabeth gave her a wry look. "It must have been. You're actually smiling, and it isn't even noon yet."

"You know those Sigmas," Celine said, removing a cigarette and tossing the pack back onto her bedside table. "They were made for fun."

163

"Um," Elizabeth said, turning again to the mirror. "That's what they say."

Celine lit up, her eyes narrowing as the smoke swirled around her. "They really are a scream, those guys," Celine said. "You know what Pete told me?"

Elizabeth was concentrating on braiding her hair. "If you mean Peter Wilbourne, I'm not really interested in anything he has to say."

Celine blew a perfect smoke ring in Elizabeth's direction. She didn't care if Elizabeth wanted to hear what Peter said or not, she was going to hear it. This, and not the party itself, was one of the reasons Celine was in such a good mood.

"Pete said that every year the Sigmas pick a 'loser' plebe—you know, some dork who couldn't make the grade if God was handing out miracles. They pretend that they're hazing him like the other plebes, but really they're just playing with him until he breaks." Celine laughed. She was almost beginning to think that Peter Wilbourne wasn't as mediocre as she'd thought. "Isn't that too much?" she shrieked. "They even put bets on how long it will take." She coughed as she inhaled the wrong way. "Usually they take pictures, you know, for their special Sigma scrapbook? But this year Pete's making a video."

Elizabeth threw down her brush and turned to face Celine. "I don't know why you think that's so funny," she fumed. "I think it's horrible."

The sight of her roommate's face, flushed with righteous indignation, made Celine laugh even more. "Oh, but I haven't told you the best part!" she screeched. "The best part is that this year's loser is none other than your little friend Winston Egghead!"

Celine was still laughing as Elizabeth stormed out of the room, slamming the door behind her.

"Yes," Celine said, reaching for another cigarette. "Yes, I am in a very good mood this morning."

It's all coming back to me, Jessica thought as she slid another tray of dirty dishes into the kitchen hatch. *The reason I didn't last long as a waitress was that it's boring, it's demeaning, and it's* hard.

All she did for hours on end was walk back and forth through the crowded restaurant, balancing heavy trays and trying to avoid the groping hands of the more Neanderthal fraternity guys who seemed to think her job was to flirt with them.

And that was the good part. The bad part was having to stand there, smiling pleasantly, while people changed their minds five million times and talked to you as though you had the brains of a carp. If she had to serve one more customer with an attitude, she was going to have an accident with a cup of coffee. "Oh, I'm so sorry," she'd say in a whispery, innocent voice. "Clumsy me."

Over in the corner booth, someone was trying to catch her eye. Jessica's heart relocated itself somewhere around her ankles. She had seen Peter Wilbourne III, the Greek Geek, and Celine Boudreaux, the Southern Belle from Hell, come in, but they had been sitting at the other waitress's table. Sometime between Jessica's last two orders, Peter and Celine had changed tables and were now sitting at one of hers. It couldn't be a coincidence, not with those two. Neither Peter nor Celine got up in the morning before deciding whose day they were going to ruin.

"My feet ache, I've broken two nails, I haven't had time for a glass of water all afternoon, and now *this*," Jessica grumbled as she put on a happy face and headed toward the gruesome twosome.

"It's about time," Peter snapped as Jessica stopped in front of him and Celine.

Jessica took out her pad and pen. "I'm sorry," she said in her best the-customer-is-always-right voice. "It's been a very busy afternoon."

"I guess that's what it's like when you're a poor little working girl," murmured Celine, not looking up from her menu.

Peter stretched his arm across the back of the booth, his hand dangling loosely over Celine's shoulder. "What'll it be?"

Celine made a face that Jessica already recognized as the face of indecision. "Well . . ." she drawled, "the spinach salad looks good . . ." She sighed. "But the grilled cheese and sun-dried tomatoes with cilantro looks good, too . . ." She leaned against

Peter. "What do you think?" she asked him coyly. "Do you think the taquitos might be a little oily for a snack?"

Peter smiled down at her as though she were adorable. "Gee," he said, "I really don't know. Just get whatever you feel like."

The first time she made up her mind, Celine felt like the Greek melt. The second time, she felt like the chicken saté. Jessica lost interest after she'd crossed out the third order.

While Celine went through every item on the menu, and Peter kept shrugging and saying "Gee, I don't know," Jessica locked her body so that she wouldn't smack Celine on the head with her notebook.

At last, Celine threw down her menu with a triumphant flourish. "All right," she declared. "This time I really have made up my mind."

Jessica lifted her pencil, ready to try again.

"I'll have a triple espresso, but don't let it sit on the counter, it has to be hot, a glass of iced tap water with a very thin sliver of lemon in it, and a prosciutto and mozzarella on focaccia, hold the oil, with just a teensy bit of fresh basil."

She'd lost Jessica somewhere around the thin sliver of lemon. "Huh?" Jessica asked.

Peter leered at her. "Oh, come on," he said, "you're a Theta girl, aren't you? You should be able to handle a simple order. Or is it only your sister who's smart?"

167

Don't say anything, Jessica warned herself. *Just play dumb. Keep a smile on your lips, and your mouth shut.*

She was still smiling when she returned fifteen minutes later with their food.

"A Coke and blue cheese burger," she said in her most efficient voice as she set a plate in front of Peter. "And for you . . ." Jessica met Celine's eyes. "A strong coffee, a glass of polluted water with a hint of lemon, and a dry ham and cheese with a couple of dead leaves."

"You don't seem so excited about it anymore," Nina said from the depths of her closet. "What happened?"

Elizabeth stared into the closet and shrugged at the gap in shirts and dresses that she figured was Nina. "Nothing happened. I had a great time on the date, and I was really excited the next morning, but I don't know . . ."

She lapsed into silence, trying to analyze her own vague feelings about her night out with William White. She had had fun—more than that, really. She'd relaxed and totally enjoyed herself.

Even now it seemed impossible that she had gone out with someone who wasn't Todd Wilkins and hadn't thought about Todd for as much as a second. Not once had she thought, *Todd wouldn't say that . . .* or *Todd wouldn't do that . . .* or *Todd would never have ordered that . . .* For the first time in a long time, she hadn't heard another man laugh or watched him smile and missed Todd.

"It's really strange," Elizabeth said at last. "When I'm with William, I think he's really nice and attractive and everything. But when I haven't seen him for a day or two, I start thinking that he isn't quite as nice as he seems."

Nina emerged from the closet with an armload of clothes. "Nerves," she pronounced, dumping her load on the bed beside Elizabeth. "You like him, but you're afraid to like him too much because you don't want to get hurt again."

Elizabeth laughed. "You know, in the hands of some people Psych 1 can be a dangerous thing."

"Actually," Nina said in a mock-serious voice, "I did Psych 1 in summer school two years ago. This is Psych 251.3, Behavioral Patterns and Responses." She smiled. "Which gives me the authority to say that you, my friend, are a classic case."

Elizabeth smiled back, but she was still thoughtful. "I suppose it could be true," she admitted slowly. "It doesn't make sense that I should go hot and cold like this, does it? William is an incredible person; you can tell that just by looking at him."

"Incredible?" Nina echoed. "You could say that. He makes most people on this campus look like visitors from the Planet of the Nerds."

While Nina sorted through the clothes she'd taken from the closet, Elizabeth considered what she'd said. Maybe Nina and Psych 251.3 were right. Maybe it was that she was afraid of being hurt again. Why else should she feel so ambivalent?

Losing Todd had been one of the hardest things Elizabeth had ever had to face. There were still times when she missed him so much she could cry; and there were still times she couldn't believe he really was gone. She certainly didn't want to go through all that pain and rejection again.

Nina lifted a flowing aquamarine skirt from the pile. She held it up in front of her. "Unless, of course, it's Tom Watts," she said quietly.

Elizabeth concentrated her attention on the skirt. She didn't want to talk about Tom Watts. Not now or ever. It was obvious to her that she'd completely deluded herself into thinking he might care about her. Everyone knew that Tom Watts cared about nothing but work and WSVU. How could she have been so dumb as to think that he'd poured out his heart in a poem to her?

Tom didn't have a heart. He had a conscience, he had drive, motivation, and an admirable sense of right and justice, but he didn't have a heart. Not the kind that most men had. Not the kind of heart that let in anything like love.

"I like that skirt," Elizabeth said, tilting her head to one side appraisingly. "It's simple but classic." She took hold of the hem of the filmy fabric. "What would you wear it with?"

Much to Elizabeth's relief, Nina took the hint. "I don't know." She held the skirt at arm's length,

170

her expression indecisive. "Is this right for a BSU banquet, I ask myself? I don't want to feel completely out of place."

"It looks fine to me," Elizabeth said. "What do you think is wrong with it? Too plain? Too fancy? Too heavy? Too light?" She grinned at her friend. "Or too subdued to be seen in sitting next to the devastating Bryan Nelson?"

Nina shook her head slowly. "Too white," she said.

Elizabeth laughed in surprise. She started to point out that the skirt wasn't white, it was blue, when she realized what Nina meant.

"Too *white*?" Elizabeth asked. "What are you talking about, Nina? How can it be too white? It's just a skirt."

"That's the problem, isn't it? This is a black function, Elizabeth. I don't want to look like I'm dining with the Thetas." Nina threw the skirt onto a chair and picked up a dark orange dress from the heap of clothes on the bed. "Let's face it," she went on. "*You* could wear that skirt."

"I think you're getting a little paranoid," Elizabeth said. "What do you think everybody else is going to be wearing? Batik dashikis and turbans?"

"Well . . ." Nina mumbled.

Elizabeth couldn't help smiling. "Nina, believe me, they'll probably all be in suits and evening dresses. And so what if they aren't? People have different styles. You should wear what you're comfortable in, what you normally wear."

Nina appraised the orange dress glumly. "Are you sure?" she asked, sounding completely unconfident in Elizabeth's opinion. "My mother says that people in organizations like this—"

"Your mother worries too much," Elizabeth said. "And about the wrong things, if you ask me."

Nina pretended she couldn't imagine what Elizabeth was talking about. "What do you mean, 'the wrong things'?" she asked.

Elizabeth gave Nina a teasing smile. "Well, if I were your mother, I wouldn't worry that you were going to a BSU banquet or that you were about to turn into a political radical," she said. "I'd worry that you were going out with a man who makes William White look like a visitor from the Planet of the Nerds. Who knows? You might even forget about studying for a whole night."

Laughing, Nina threw the orange dress at Elizabeth's head.

"Don't worry," she said. "I'm bringing my chem homework with me. That way, when everyone else is falling asleep over the after-dinner speeches, I'll have something to do."

Let Steven Wakefield come after me tonight with all his moral indignation, Jessica thought as she turned the Karmann Ghia into the parking lot of her apartment complex. *I'll run him over.*

What a rotten day she'd had! There didn't seem

to be a bone in her body that didn't ache. Her feet and legs ached because she'd been standing on them for hours. Her arms and shoulders ached because she'd been hauling those heavy trays. The rest of her simply ached out of sympathy.

Wincing slightly, Jessica turned off the ignition and climbed out from behind the wheel. Fortunately, there was no sign of her brother either outside the building or peering from behind the curtains of his living room window.

It wasn't until she reached her own hallway that she realized she'd been so busy all afternoon, she hadn't thought of Mike at all. She stopped at the top of the stairs, astounded at herself. How could she? Not thinking about Mike for an entire afternoon was like forgetting to breathe. Since the first moment she set eyes on him, that afternoon that she'd rear-ended his Corvette, not an hour had gone by when he hadn't entered her mind.

That just shows you how unsuited I am for manual labor, she told herself as she took out her key and slid it into their lock. *If I had to do that job eight hours a day, five days a week, I'd probably forget my own name.*

"Mike!" she called as she entered the apartment. "Honey, what's left of me is home!"

There was no answer. Jessica looked around. The living room was exactly as it had been when she'd left that morning. There was no sign that anyone had been back since then: no newspaper on the coffee table, no shoes taken off by the sofa, no music playing on the stereo.

She threw herself onto the sofa, fighting back the tears. It was unbelievable. It was more than unbelievable, it was some kind of cruel cosmic joke. Here she'd had one of the worst days of her life—a day she would happily have traded for a day in the life of some girl who was short and dumpy and couldn't get a date—and now it had just gotten considerably worse.

It wasn't only that she'd been looking forward to telling Mike about her first day at work, but now she was going to have to spend the whole night worrying about where he was, and wondering if it were her fault that he hadn't come home.

Jessica closed her eyes, hoping that when she opened them again she would find that she'd been dreaming. Lying silent and still on the couch, she was suddenly aware of a peculiar aroma. Jessica sniffed. Yes, there really was a strange smell in the apartment—mango, or papaya maybe, something lush and sensual like that. She opened her eyes. The apartment was still empty, so as far as she could tell she hadn't been dreaming, but she could still smell that ripe, fruity aroma.

"Mike?" she called again, slowly getting up from the sofa. "Mike, are you here?"

She listened. Very, very faintly, she thought she heard the sound of a stereo playing something delicate and soothing. "Mike?" Jessica called

174

again. "Are you playing games with me?"

She tiptoed over to the bedroom door and opened it slowly. The bedroom was just as she'd left it that morning, too, her clothes in a heap on one side of the bed, his hanging neatly on the back of the closet. But she could hear the music, still faint but nearer and definite.

"Mike?" she called again. "Come on, Mike, you're scaring me."

The bathroom door was ajar. "I know you're in there!" she shouted.

Suddenly, that warm rich laugh filled up the room.

"You want me, you're gonna have to come and get me!" he shouted back.

Jessica raced to the bathroom and wrenched open the door. "Mike, what—" Her words stopped abruptly as she looked around. There was candlelight, a steaming tub of mango-scented bubbles, Mike's portable tape deck playing one of her favorite songs, and Mike himself, standing there with his arms opened wide.

"I thought my working girl might like a nice relaxing bath and a back rub after her first day," he said, taking her into his arms. "Plus I've made your favorite pasta for supper." He ran a row of kisses across her forehead. "I thought you might like to be taken care of tonight."

"Oh, Mike," Jessica moaned. "I have a Theta meeting—"

He gently began to massage her back. "Come

on, Jess," he murmured. "You don't want to waste the little time we have together hanging around with those snobs."

Jessica's bones didn't ache anymore. They were melting, melting away with her bad day and her troubles. All she wanted to do was collapse into his arms forever and ever.

"I thought you loved me," Mike said. "Was I wrong? Do you care about them more than me?"

She didn't need much persuasion; and she didn't need to think to know the answer to his question.

"You know I love you," she whispered back. "It's just that—"

"Come on," he insisted. "You get in that tub and relax while you tell me about your day, and then I'll give you the massage to end all massages. How does that sound?"

Jessica leaned back, looking into his eyes. "It sounds wonderful," she admitted, secretly wondering how she was going to square another missed Theta evening with Alison Quinn. Maybe she could have her bath and then go. There was still plenty of time.

"You should keep clear of that Peter Wilbourne character," Mike said after she told him about her run-in with Peter and Celine. "I don't like him."

Jessica, drifting in a mango sea with Mike sitting on the floor beside her, watched the candlelight flickering on the walls. "Sometimes I think he's the only one who likes him," she said.

"No, I mean it, Jess."

There was something in Mike's voice that made her look over at him. "He's bad news. Him and that other character."

Jessica sat up a little, leaning on the side of the tub. "What other character?"

"You know, the blond."

Jessica started to smile. Blonds weren't exactly an endangered species in Southern California, especially not on the SVU campus. Suddenly, though, she knew exactly whom he meant. "William White?" she asked.

Mike nodded. "Yeah, William White. Promise me you'll stay away from both of them, but especially him. There's something not right about that guy."

"You don't have to worry about me," Jessica said, sinking back into the suds. "I don't even know him. I don't even know anyone who knows him."

Nina was wrong. No one fell asleep during the after-dinner speeches. Instead, everyone listened, riveted with attention and interest. And no one was more riveted than Nina.

Her brain was spinning. So many things had been discussed that she hadn't really thought about before. She'd always been told that the people who didn't make it in the world were people who didn't want to work. That they were lazy, or stupid, or expected everyone else to give them a living.

After hearing Dr. Springwater, one of the people and scientists she most admired, tell of his boyhood in a New York ghetto, where just existing from one day to the next was a major struggle and getting through high school and college was nothing short of a miracle, she was beginning to see that things weren't as black and white as she'd thought.

Bryan tapped his spoon against her water glass when the last speech was over. "Does that slightly dazed expression mean you've had a good time?" he asked, illuminating their side of the room with his smile.

Nina smiled back. "Yes," she said. "It does. I'm really glad I came—I've learned a lot."

He laughed. "You should have seen your face when we first sat down. You looked like you thought everybody was going to be wearing Malcolm X baseball caps and waving guns."

Nina blushed, unable to stop from laughing herself. "Of course I didn't," she said, deciding not to mention that she'd imagined everyone would be wearing native African dress. "I knew everybody here was going to be totally normal. But my mother sort of thought there might be a few of what she calls 'that element' here."

The dazzling eyes shone with humor. "You should've told her that my father couldn't make it tonight, so she didn't have to worry." He leaned closer. "But you're wrong about everyone being normal," he whispered in a Boris Karloff voice. "There's nothing normal about me. I put ketchup on my cornflakes."

"Oh, stop it." She shoved him away. "Nobody puts ketchup on their cornflakes."

He nodded. "I do, I swear I do. Tell your mother, all us black troublemakers put ketchup on our cornflakes."

Nina was feeling so happy and relaxed that she had to resist the urge to give him a hug. How long had it been since she'd enjoyed herself this much?

A niggling thought made her frown. She wasn't sure that she'd ever enjoyed herself this much.

"I haven't actually mentioned you to my mother," Nina admitted. "I thought I'd spare her the terrible truth that I know someone with such unsavory eating habits."

His face became suddenly serious. "How come?" he asked, looking at her quizzically.

"How come what?"

"How come you didn't tell her you were coming to the banquet with me?"

Nina shrugged, suddenly uncomfortable. Why hadn't she mentioned Bryan to her mother? Her parents wouldn't mind that she was going out with a guy. Even one whose father marched on Washington. Especially since they weren't *really* going out. They were just pals, that was all. They were both good at chemistry. Her parents knew as well as she did that she didn't have time for anything serious at this point in her life.

"No special reason," she finally answered. "I just didn't. I don't tell them about every friend I have."

Bryan nodded. "Sure," he said. "You're an adult, you're entitled to your privacy." He leaned back in his chair and lifted his coffee cup to his lips. "I told my old man about you."

Nina turned so fast, her beads knocked against his shoulder. "What did you tell him?" she demanded.

Bryan tugged at one of her braids. "I told him you were one of those 'white' black girls he was always warning me against."

The room was dark, smoky, crowded, and noisy. As far as Winston could tell, everyone but him and one or two of the other plebes whose turn hadn't come yet was drunk.

He could tell they were drunk not so much because they seemed to be having such a good time, but because whenever someone laughed or got up from his seat, something spilled or someone else fell over.

Winston looked warily around, pretending that he wasn't, pretending that he was fully into the swing of the party and having a great Sigma time. Thank goodness he'd had the forethought to switch his almost-full beers for the empty mugs of the guy next to him before the Death Punch Ritual began.

"Chug! Chug! Chug! Chug!" the Sigmas shouted as the plebe a few seats away from Winston stood up, raising the glass of Death Punch to his lips.

"Chug! Chug! Chug! Chug!" they roared, whooping and hollering and slapping the table so hard that it shook.

Feeling foolish, Winston chanted along. He shouldn't be here. In his heart he knew that he shouldn't be here. It wasn't fun. It wasn't even close to fun. It was dumb. Two of the plebes had already passed out, and another one had barfed all over the floor.

Peter Wilbourne, swaying like something hanging in the wind, got to his feet. "It's Winnie-the-Pooh's turn!" he bellowed. "Come on, Winnie! Take the glass."

Bill, one of the Sigmas Winston used to think was his friend, handed him the chalice of Death Punch.

"Way to go, Win!" Bill shouted.

Winston raised the cup to his lips. It smelled like formaldehyde. He took a tentative sip. Well, that was all right, he told himself, it tasted exactly the way he would have expected formaldehyde to taste.

"Chug! Chug! Chug! Chug!" the Sigmas yelled. "Chugchugchugchug!"

Winston started to chug. His immediate reaction was to spit out the vile concoction, but aware of all the bloodshot eyes that were watching him, he forced it down.

"Chugchugchugchugchugchug!"

The good thing was, the more you drank, the easier it was to drink more.

Bill took the empty cup away and handed him another. "Way to go, Winnie," he said again.

The small part of Winston's brain that wasn't already paralyzed knew that this wasn't right. All the other plebes had drunk only one cup of Death Punch. He looked around.

"Go on, boy!" Peter Wilbourne yelled. "You're not through yet!"

That's not true, Winston thought as he looked into the garishly pink liquid. *I am through. I am definitely through.* And then he passed out.

Chapter Nine

Winston Egbert, sitting by himself in a corner of the cafeteria, groaned. It wasn't a particularly loud groan—he didn't have the strength for a really loud one—but it was audible. A few people at nearby tables glanced over. Winston didn't care. The only thing he cared about this morning was which disaster was likely to happen to him first.

Was the smell of the food on the tray in front of him going to make him throw up? Was the remorseless din made by hundreds of pieces of cutlery being scraped against china going to make his brain explode? Or was the unusual intensity of the sun this morning going to make him blind even though he still had on his sunglasses?

Vomit? Winston wondered, trying not to breathe because the movement upset his stomach. *Exploding brain? Blindness? All three at once?* But his feeble attempts to grapple with the question came to an abrupt stop when he realized that someone was call-ing his name. Shouting his name, to be more pre-cise. Someone with a shrill, grating voice was shouting his name over a loudspeaker at top volume.

Very slowly and carefully, Winston raised his head. The shrill, grating voice belonged to Denise Waters. As far as he could tell, as he squinted through his extra-dark shades, she wasn't actually hooked up to a loudspeaker. Behind her were Anoushka and Debbie, and they were all talking at once. They looked painfully energetic and cheerful.

"Morning, Winnie!" they all yelled as they reached his table.

Not even bothering to ask if he wanted any company, they started dragging out chairs and slamming down their trays. It sounded to Winston like a building being demolished.

"Listen, you guys," Winston whispered. "Do you think you could be a little more quiet? Please?"

"What's with you, Winnie?" Anoushka roared. "Did you get up on the wrong side of bed?"

Denise laughed. Normally, Denise's laugh re-minded Winston of tiny glass bells tinkling against each other in a gentle breeze, but today it sounded more like cannon fire at close range.

"It looks to me like Winnie has a hangover," Denise boomed. "And a pretty bad one, judging from the greenish color of his skin."

Denise, Anoushka, and Debbie all cackled.

He wanted to beg them again not to make so much noise, but a new wave of nausea had him in its grip. Not only were the girls making enough of a racket to wake up the dinosaurs, they were eating. They were eating eggs, and bacon, and something that smelled suspiciously like liver. Fried liver. Winston clamped his mouth shut.

"What's behind these shades?" Debbie asked. She leaned over and lifted the sunglasses from Winston's eyes. Her breath smelled like boiled eggs.

Winston winced. "Stop that," he managed to whine. "What are you trying to do, blind me?"

Denise peered into his face. "Anybody in there?" she teased.

Normally, nothing made Winston happier than looking into Denise Waters's beautiful eyes, but today he might as well have been staring into a septic tank. "No," Winston moaned, pulling the shades back in place. "There's nobody home."

"Sounds like another great Sigma hazing party to me." Anoushka whistled. "What did the big guys make you do? Chug three gallons of kerosene?"

Winston shuddered. That was frighteningly close to the truth.

"It was nothing like that," he lied. "It's just that the sun's very strong this morning. I think there must be a hole in the ozone layer right over SVU."

Denise laughed again. This time her laugh reminded him of excited bats. "There's a hole all right," she said, banging her coffee cup down on the table, "but it isn't in the ozone layer, it's in your head."

"Denise is right," Debbie said, breathing the liver from a dead calf all over him. "Why don't you wise up, Winnie, and dump those guys?"

"Because they're my friends," he muttered. "They're my buddies."

To Winston's left some large, wild creature—a tiger, maybe, or a wild boar—crunched through the bones of something innocent and defenseless. Winston looked over. Anoushka was chewing her toast.

"It's more like they're your enemies," Anoushka said. "If you hang out with these guys much longer, you're going to be scarred for life."

"Assuming you live long enough to have a life," Denise said.

Jessica was just going into the employees' washroom to clean up before she left her shift when a group of Thetas came into the coffeehouse. Standing frozen in the doorway, Jessica watched the laughing gaggle of girls burst through the entrance in a cloud of expensive perfume. Alison Quinn was at the center of the group.

As much as she didn't want them to see her, Jessica couldn't quite pull away. They were all carrying brightly colored bags, and from what she overheard as they waited to be seated, they'd just come back from shopping.

Alison Quinn's loud, confident voice brayed across the foyer. "I'm so glad I found that lavender suit," she was saying. "I do feel it's important to look really right for the Theta swearing-in ceremony." She smiled as though she'd just received a round of applause. "One wants to look serious, of course, but also elegant."

Jessica caught her breath. The Theta swearing-in ceremony! She'd been so busy with school, work, and Mike that she'd actually forgotten about the most important event in her life, the night she became a full-fledged Theta. Tomorrow night.

"Where is the waiter?" Alison demanded, looking around with a bored expression. "We don't have all afternoon to stand here."

Jessica pushed into the washroom and locked the door behind her. Outside, she could hear Artie Stigman himself showing the Thetas to a table while Alison complained that she didn't want the one in the corner.

Still standing with her back against the door, Jessica stared glumly at her reflection in the mirror. She couldn't help wondering if she'd forgotten about the induction ceremony kind of on purpose. Mike wanted her to dump the Thetas, anyway. "Why do you want to hang out with that bunch of snobs when you have me?" he'd said yesterday morning. "How come I'm not enough for you?"

At first she'd argued with him that being a

Theta was something she'd dreamed of all through high school, that there was no way she'd consider giving them up. But lately Jessica had begun to wonder if Mike was right. She had to admit that when you got down to basics, the Thetas weren't really that important. Mike was important: living with him, being with him, making him happy.

Jessica sighed. Right at this moment, however, she wasn't sure of anything. Except that she felt awful.

In all her eighteen years, this was the first time Jessica had ever looked in a mirror and not had a reason to smile: her shining golden hair, her sparkling blue-green eyes, her infectious smile. But she wasn't smiling now. Her hair was limp and stringy, her eyes were ringed by dark circles, and she smelled like mocha rum, the flavor of the milk shake one of the other waiters had accidentally spilled all over her earlier.

Look at you, Jessica said to herself. *You go to school, you go to work, and you're starting to look like Cinderella before she met her fairy godmother.* What had happened to the fun-loving party girl she used to be? Where was Miss Social Whirl? She thought of the Thetas, all of them happy and pretty, coming back from shopping with time to spend just sitting around the coffeehouse.

She raised her chin, her eyes sparking with their old fire and determination. "You should stay in the Thetas," she told herself sternly. "You should go home, take a nice hot bath, get dressed in something that doesn't have food stains on it, and go over to Theta house tonight to see what plans have been made for tomorrow." She nodded at her reflection. "You're going to get back in the swing of things before it's too late."

Jessica sang along with the radio as she drove home. Despite the traumas of the day and her aching feet, she was in a good mood. As happy as she was with Mike, she was still looking forward to dressing up a little and getting out of the house for a few hours to hang out with other girls.

The song changed to one of Mike's favorites, and Jessica's mood changed with it. Mike hated to come home and find the apartment empty and a note telling him that she'd be back later. He said it reminded him of his mother. When he was a kid, his mother was always out. She'd promise to spend the evening with him, but then he'd come home from school and find a note on the table saying, *See you later, honey. I won't be late.* Mike said his mother was always late; sometimes hours, sometimes months.

Jessica made a sudden left and headed the Karmann Ghia in the direction of Mike's garage. He wouldn't be so upset if she told him in person. Besides, it would give her a chance to talk to him. She parked at the end of his street. *And a chance to kiss him,* she added as she walked to the garage.

Jessica could hear Mike's laugh as she reached the garage. Just as she was about to call out to him, she heard another laugh. The second laugh belonged to a woman.

Not even thinking about what she was doing, Jessica moved toward the building and slowed down, almost tiptoeing the rest of the way. She peered around the corner of the garage. Mike was at the back with a tall redhead wearing a leather motorcycle jacket. The two of them were squatting beside a large black-and-green bike. Their shoulders were touching and their heads close together as they examined something.

Don't start jumping to conclusions again, Jessica warned herself. *He's just fixing her motorcycle, that's all. People can laugh when they're fixing a motorcycle.*

The redhead said something and Mike turned to look at her. There was one unbearable second when Jessica was sure Mike and the redhead were going to kiss, but then he caught sight of her.

"Baby!" Mike cried. "What a nice surprise."

Jessica's eyes met the redhead's. The redhead didn't seem to think that "nice" was the right word either.

Tom was nodding as Elizabeth moved the mouse to highlight information on the computer screen.

"I see what you're getting at," he said. "You

definitely think there's a link between this mysterious 'secret society' and the fraternity hazing deaths."

Elizabeth beamed at him. Part of the pleasure of working with someone as intelligent as Tom was that she never had to waste any time trying to explain how her mind worked. He was always right there, anticipating the next step.

"It has to be," Elizabeth said excitedly. "Every seven years there's an 'accidental' death, and at about the same time or immediately after there's a spate of strange occurrences that don't seem related to anything." She scrolled backward. "Look what happened seven years ago."

Tom leaned forward on his elbows, his expression intense. "'A Sigma pledge falls into the swimming pool and drowns,'" he read, surveying the areas she had highlighted. "'Several minority shops near the campus are vandalized and forced to shut down. The controversial left-wing head of the sociology department resigns suddenly. A peaceful demonstration concerning homosexual rights on campus ends in violence, and afterward the leader of the demonstration disappears . . .'"

Elizabeth nudged him. "See what I'm getting at?"

"Sure I do." His voice became thoughtful. "You're guessing there's got to be some link between all those events, right? You think somebody is trying to control things on and around the campus."

"More than that," Elizabeth said. "I think that

whoever it is uses the hazing deaths as a distraction."

"Distraction?" Tom looked over, a shocked understanding showing in his eyes. "You mean the campus goes into an uproar over the death and no one notices all the other things that are going on?"

Elizabeth nodded. "Elementary, my dear Watson."

But Tom was shaking his head. "Just hold on a second, Sherlock. It's a good hunch—and it's a hunch I'd be inclined to go with, especially when you put it up against the other years." He turned and looked her in the eyes. "But a hunch is all it is. Face it, at any given time in any given year you're going to have stories like this."

"But not a fraternity death, and not with such a regular pattern," Elizabeth argued.

"I admit that," Tom conceded. "But you still haven't come up with any theory as to *why*." He leaned back, his eyes on the screen. "Why a spurt of activity every seven years . . . that's what we have to find out. Why not every year, or every two years . . . ?"

"We?" Elizabeth couldn't keep the smile from her face. "Did you say that's what *we* have to find out?"

Tom nodded. "I can't let you start snooping around on your own, can I?" He shifted in his chair. "I don't want anything to happen to you," he added in a mumble.

Since she discovered the real author of the poem, Elizabeth had managed to put her secret thoughts about Tom out of her head and heart. But at the words "I don't want anything to happen to you" they came rushing back with a force that scared her. *Don't start getting any ideas,* Elizabeth warned herself. *He doesn't mean anything by that.*

"You mean because I'm too valuable a reporter?" she asked.

Still facing the screen, Tom mumbled something else.

"What?" Elizabeth asked.

He glanced over at her so quickly that she couldn't quite determine the look in his eyes. "Why don't we get out of here?" he suddenly asked. "Let's take a drive by the coast, clear our heads. Maybe we'll come up with some more ideas. I know a nice place where we could get something to eat."

Yes! The word was screaming through Elizabeth's brain. *Yes! Yes! Yes!* She couldn't think of anything she'd rather do than drive along the shore with Tom Watts on a night bright with stars. Elizabeth opened her mouth to answer.

"Well?" Tom asked. "What do you say?"

"No." Elizabeth hadn't meant to sound so final and abrupt, but she was so surprised that the answer wasn't yes, it came out that way. It was only as she started to speak that she remembered she had a date with William tonight.

That cold, withdrawn look came over Tom

immediately and he turned away.

"It's just that I have other plans," Elizabeth said hastily. "It's something I can't change."

"I guess there are a lot of things in this world that can't be changed," Tom said.

"Listen to me!" Nina said, laughing as she set down her tray at a table in the middle of the snack bar. "I haven't stopped talking since we left the meeting."

Bryan slid into the seat next to hers. "Yes, you have," he assured her. He took one of her fries and popped it into his mouth. "There were a few minutes of silence while you debated between the black bean burrito and the cheddar cheese burger. There were at least five seconds of silence when you dropped your fork." He took another fry and pointed it at her. "And you did let me get in at least seven words while we were leaving the meeting."

Nina blushed. She couldn't remember a time when she'd ever behaved like this, but for some reason she was practically bubbling with excitement. "I don't know what's gotten into me. I don't usually rattle on like this."

Bryan made an exaggerated face of understanding. "Sure you don't, Nina. You're usually very quiet and a great listener."

"But I am," Nina protested. She shook ketchup onto her plate. "There was something about that meeting, though . . ."

It was three nights after the BSU banquet, and Nina had planned to put in a solid night of work. But Bryan had caught her just as she was entering the library and she'd let him persuade her to go to the weekly BSU meeting with him.

Bryan grinned at her over his soda. "You mean like maybe it was interesting and stimulating?" he teased.

Nina felt herself blush again. She couldn't decide which was embarrassing her more, the fact that she couldn't stop blushing, or the fact that she couldn't shut up.

"Yes," Nina agreed. "Like maybe it was interesting and stimulating." She picked up her burger. "You know," she said slowly, trying to get her thoughts together, "all through high school I believed that the only important thing was academic success. I thought that as long as you did your schoolwork, you'd know everything you needed to know. But after tonight . . ." Nina shrugged. After tonight, she knew that there was more to knowledge than the facts in a textbook. Her brain was moving so fast in so many new directions that she could hardly keep up with it.

Bryan was smiling at her. "I told you you'd like the BSU, didn't I?" he asked. "I may look like the kind of guy your mother won't let in the house, but really I'm a very sound dude at heart."

Nina decided not to think too much about Bryan and her mother. "It's just that I thought things were so simple. You know. But after hearing that discussion on economic racism . . . Well, I guess hard work just isn't enough."

"And I guess that even though you look like the kind of girl my old man would ban from his apartment, you're really pretty sound, too."

"Thanks." Nina grinned, trying to avoid looking too deeply into those eyes.

Bryan reached across the table and touched her hand. "So what happens now?" he asked.

Nina looked at their hands, dark against the white Formica tabletop. The spot where his hand met hers felt as warm as sunshine. "What happens now?"

"Yeah, what happens now." His fingers folded over hers. "I can't keep asking you to BSU stuff so I can see you, since you're a member now, too. So what I want to know is, where do we go from here?"

"Well, I . . ." It wasn't as though Nina hadn't thought about Bryan practically every waking hour since the BSU dinner. She'd done more than think about him. She'd watched him in class, she'd looked out for him when she was walking on the campus, she'd even imagined him holding her hand, just the way he was holding it now. But she didn't know what to say. She'd never had time for a boyfriend, and even if she had, Bryan Nelson was very definitely not the guy her parents would have chosen for her. "I don't know . . ."

He leaned closer, his handsome face serious. "You don't know if you want to go out with me, or you don't know if your parents would want you to go out with me?"

Nina opened her mouth and closed it again. Her parents wouldn't have wanted her to join the Black Students Union either, but she'd already done that. That was what growing up was all about: starting to make your own decisions; starting to take responsibility for your life.

"Well?" Bryan prompted.

She took his hand and squeezed it. "You want to go to the movies with me some night?" she asked.

Winston strode into the coffeehouse in his best impersonation of a Sigma brother. His hands were jammed in his pockets, his sunglasses were in place, the collar of his jacket was turned up, and his head was held high. Despite the difficulty of seeing in the dark café with his shades on, he scanned the room with the bored and slightly haughty expression that Peter Wilbourne had made popular.

Winston squinted into the distance, looking for Todd. Pretending to be brushing some dust off the lenses, he lifted his glasses. There, in a corner, was Todd studying the menu. Winston's heart leapt with relief. At last he had another man to tell his troubles to.

Since the beginning of the year, Winston had discovered that there were advantages to living with women. First of all, women were a lot more fun to look at than most of the guys he knew. Second, they liked to be helpful and always had supplies of food and coffee handy. Third, they would listen to your problems.

But there were disadvantages, too. The biggest, as far as Winston was concerned, was that the women he lived with didn't understand about fraternities. He was tired of arguing with every girl on his floor about whether he should or should not bail out of the Sigmas. He could argue till he was blue in the face, but the women of Oakley Hall refused to listen to reason. "The Sigmas are a bunch of morons," they kept telling him. "Grow up."

That's why Winston wanted to talk to Todd. He needed to talk to someone who understood about bonding rituals and the male sense of fun. Todd was perfect. Todd belonged to a fraternity, Todd was a major jock, and—best of all—Todd was a man.

"So how is it going?" Winston asked as he took his seat. "You and Mark Gathers aren't worried about all this uproar over the athletic department, are you?"

"No, we're cool." Todd shook his head. "And anyway, if you want my opinion, I'm pretty sure the whole thing will die down by itself. The university will have an inquiry, but it's going to be hard for them to prove anything. Especially about the players. I mean, we just took what was offered;

it's not like we asked for special treatment, is it?"

"Of course not," Winston agreed. "It doesn't seem like you did anything wrong."

"Exactly," Todd said. "All the TV spot did was make a big deal about nothing."

Winston ducked behind his menu. "Are you mad at Elizabeth for doing the story in the first place?" he asked cautiously.

At the mention of Elizabeth a strange expression flickered in Todd's eyes. "Elizabeth?" he asked. "No, I'm not mad at Elizabeth. She told me what she was doing beforehand and I told her to go ahead." Todd laughed wryly. "What surprises me is that everybody made such a big deal of it. I didn't think people would take her seriously."

"Women," Winston said gloomily. "They think differently than we do, don't they?"

Todd shrugged. "I guess so. I can't always figure them out."

Winston put down his menu. "It's true, though. They don't understand what's important to men."

Todd grinned. "Do I detect the moan of a man with girl problems?" he asked.

Despite Todd's jokiness, Winston could tell that he was sympathetic. He grinned back.

"It's the girls—I mean women—in my dorm," Winston said. "They think I should dump the Sigmas."

Winston was relieved by Todd's reaction. He

looked puzzled for a second, and then he burst out laughing. "Dump the Sigmas? Are they nuts?"

Winston leaned forward eagerly. "That's what I keep saying. I think they're crazy. But you know girls, they think everything that's really fun is either dangerous or stupid."

Todd nodded. "Let me guess. It's the hazing, right? They can't understand why you'd put yourself through it. They think it's pointless and idiotic."

Winston's heart felt light and joyful. There wasn't anything wrong with the Sigmas or what they were making him do. Winston was so happy, he practically felt like hugging Todd. That obviously wouldn't have been the Sigma thing to do. Sigmas only hugged each other during or after a football game.

"They all act like they're my mother," he went on. He shuddered. "I live in terror that one of them's going to go up to Peter Wilbourne and tell him to stop bullying me."

Todd shook his head. "You're right, I guess—it is their maternal instincts."

"They're totally overprotective," Winston complained. "They not only think I'm being a total dope, they think that the Sigmas are trying to kill me."

Todd's laughter rippled around them. "Kill you? Why would the Sigmas want to kill you? They like you. They've pledged you to their house."

"Well, that's what I said." Winston shook his

head. "But you know women—they have their own logic."

Todd beckoned the waiter. "Let me know if you ever figure it out."

"Now this is what I call a perfect evening," Mike said. He picked up a piece of chicken with his chopsticks and held it to Jessica's mouth. "Chinese take-out, a good video, and my baby by my side."

Jessica swallowed the chicken and gave Mike a kiss. "It is perfect, isn't it?" She was having a lot more fun than she would have if she'd spent the evening with the Thetas, that was for sure.

Mike set down the container of chicken and broccoli and put his arm around her. "You know, I was so glad to see you come into the garage this afternoon," he said softly. "It was just like we were married, you dropping by just to say hello, asking me what I wanted for dinner . . ."

"I missed you," Jessica said, snuggling against him. "I didn't want to have to wait till after you finished work to see you."

The afternoon she'd had and the decision she'd made to go to the Theta house seemed so long ago that Jessica could almost believe she was telling Mike the truth. So what if she'd only changed her mind about how she was spending her evening when she'd seen the redhead.

Mike kissed the tip of her nose. "That's what I

love about you," he whispered. "You make me feel important. I need to know that you're always there for me, baby. I don't want to share you with anyone."

"You don't have to worry about that," Jessica whispered back. "You're the most important thing in my life." She raised her head and looked into those deep, golden eyes. "You believe that, don't you? You know there could never be anyone else for me?"

"I don't want there to be *anything* else," Mike said. "I want to be everything for you." He held her gaze. "The first thing I thought when you turned up like that this afternoon was that you'd come by to tell me you were going out with your girlfriends tonight."

Jessica's heart skipped a beat. "Really?" she asked. "What made you think that?"

"I don't know." Mike shrugged. "You don't usually just visit because you were missing me. You're usually too busy."

She rubbed her nose against his. "I'm never too busy for you, and you know it."

He put on a sulky face. "Oh, yeah? What about all those sorority things you're always running off to?"

"What sorority things I'm always running off to?" Jessica asked, her voice light and teasing. She laughed. "I don't even think the Thetas remember who I am anymore." She hesitated, wondering if now would be a good time to tell him about the induction ceremony tomorrow night or not.

"That's okay with me," Mike said. His mouth brushed across her ear. "I want you all to myself."

Jessica slipped her arms around his neck. She could tell him about the ceremony in the morning, she decided. There was plenty of time for that. Right now, there were more important things on her mind. His lips moved down her cheek until they found her mouth.

Celine flicked a match past Elizabeth's head. It hit the mirror and fell to the dresser. Elizabeth, hurriedly getting ready to go out, didn't turn around.

"So we've got another heavy date with the enigmatic William White, have we?" Celine drawled. "Where are you going this time? Don't tell me the opera's in town."

"We're going to a poetry reading," Elizabeth said. "Not that it's any of your business."

Celine made a face. "Ooh, a poetry reading. Now, that sounds exciting." She stretched out on her bed. "If I didn't know you so well, I'd think it was a cover. I'd think a person could only pretend she'd rather listen to some dumb poem than have a good time."

Elizabeth glanced over her shoulder. "William and I do have a good time," she said in what Celine thought of as her I-Am-Perfect voice.

"Do you?" Celine asked, smiling at Elizabeth's face in the mirror. "And just how good a time is that? Has he put the moves on you yet, Princess? Has the lovely William slipped his hand inside your blouse?"

"You really are disgusting, you know that?" Elizabeth threw down her brush and turned around. "Unlike the subhumans you go out with, Celine, William White happens to be a gentleman. He is one of the most sensitive, considerate men I've ever met."

Celine hooted with laughter. "I'm glad I'm already lying down or I would have keeled over at that one," she gasped. "A gentleman? William? Even you can't be that naive! He's as horny as a field of rabbits." She ran her tongue over her lips. "And believe me, I know what I'm talking about."

Her roommate's reaction was even better than Celine had hoped. Elizabeth's face went crimson. "You're sick, Celine," she hissed, trying to control her temper. "You are a petty, manipulative witch. And if you think you can turn me against William with your lies . . ."

Celine pretended to be offended. "Why, Princess," she gasped, putting her hand on her heart. "How can you think such a thing? I'm just trying to protect you, that's all. An innocent young girl like you should be careful. There's a lot about this wicked world that you don't know. Just because William's blond doesn't mean he's the good guy, you know."

"I'm not listening to any more of this," Elizabeth said, picking up her bag. "You're the last person whose opinion I'd trust."

Celine smiled as the door banged behind Elizabeth. "That's what we in Psych 1 call reverse psychology," she said softly. "Back home we just call it telling the truth and making it sound like a lie." She gave herself a hug. "But whatever you call it, it works every time."

Chapter Ten

"Hey, wake up, sleeping beauty." The manager snapped his fingers in front of Jessica's eyes. "Table ten—that's you, isn't it? They've already been waiting at least five minutes. You know those sorority types; they'll be storming out in a huff if you don't get a move on."

This has got to be the worst day of my life, Jessica thought. *First a big fight with Mike over going to the induction ceremony tonight, and now this.*

"You!" the manager snapped, taking hold of her shoulders and giving her a shove. "Now!"

Jessica walked slowly toward table ten. It was a large, round table at the front of the coffeehouse, and sitting at it were Isabella and Alison and several other Thetas. Jessica took a deep breath as she got closer. So far they hadn't noticed her, but short of some miracle they were going to notice her in about a nanosecond.

"Jessica? Jessica Wakefield?" Alison's voice was wavering between laughter and disbelief.

If she'd thought for even an instant that she could get away with it, Jessica would have said that she was Elizabeth. But she knew she couldn't. Alison might have been the biggest witch this side of Oz, but she could read, and the name tag over Jessica's breast pocket didn't say Elizabeth.

She smiled in her most pleasant and professional way. "What can I get you ladies today?" she asked, directing the question at Isabella.

Isabella looked as surprised as the others, but loyal friend that she was, she recovered quickly. "I'll have the vegetable melt," she said, scanning her menu. "And an order of hot onion rings, and a mineral water."

Jessica locked the smile on her face and turned to Alison. "And what'll you have?" she asked.

Alison flung aside her menu. "I'll have an explanation, that's what I'll have. Just what do you think you're doing working *here*?"

Jessica stared back at her. *What does she think I'm doing here? Researching a sociology paper?* "I'm earning money," Jessica answered evenly. "That's why most people work."

Alison sniffed. "And is this why you've been missing all of our important functions?" she asked. "Because you'd rather be a waitress than a Theta?"

"I told you," Jessica said, amazed at how well

she was keeping her temper. "I'm working here to earn money, that's all."

"Thetas don't have to earn money," Alison purred. "We're not a sorority of poor people, you know." Her eyes went up and down Jessica, from the stains on her apron to the runs in her stockings. "Is this what you're planning to wear to the ceremony tonight? Hamburger grease and cheap stockings?"

The other girls—all except Isabella—giggled.

Jessica looked at them. The fight she'd had with Mike this morning had been because he couldn't understand why she wanted to waste her time with a bunch of cliquey sorority girls when she could be with him. Now, as Jessica stared at their expensive clothes and condescending smiles, she suddenly realized that Mike was right. The Thetas weren't the wonderful, exciting, interesting girls Jessica had convinced herself they were.

Isabella was her only real friend among them. The rest of them were boring snobs, just as Mike said. They were petty, self-congratulating, and vain—and Alison Quinn was the worst of them all.

"Actually, I'm not planning to come tonight," Jessica said. She could feel Isabella's eyes on her, but she kept looking straight at Alison. "I'd rather wash dishes all night than go to your stupid ceremony."

"I'd say that that's probably what you will be doing," the girl next to Isabella said.

"You know what this means, don't you?"

Alison asked coldly. "You know there's no way we're going to make you a Theta sister after this."

Jessica smiled her first real smile of the day. "At last," she said. "My luck is changing."

Elizabeth looked at her sandwich as though it might bite her. "Six hundred calories? Are you *sure*?"

Her head bent over the tiny book in her hands, Nina nodded. "Pretty sure. Cheese, turkey, lettuce and tomato, brown bread . . . that's at least five hundred right there." She looked up. "Mayonnaise or butter?"

Elizabeth pulled up one corner. "Thousand Island dressing."

Nina whistled. "Oh, you are in trouble. Even mayonnaise has fewer calories than that." She flipped some pages of her book. "How many tablespoons?"

Elizabeth lifted the top slice of bread completely. "How am I supposed to know? I didn't make this sandwich. I took it from the counter."

"That's why I stick to fruit and cheese and crackers," Nina said. "It's easier to count."

Elizabeth sighed. "I know, but I'm so tired of dry toast and dry salads . . ." She stared glumly at the sandwich. "My diet's been going all right lately. One sandwich with a tiny bit of Thousand Island on it isn't going to set me back too much."

Nina shut her book. "I've been on my plateau for ages now, and I'm sure it's because of that BSU dinner." She puffed up her cheeks. "One

210

helping of roasted potatoes and it's the incredible swelling blimp again."

Elizabeth laughed. The truth was, Nina wasn't the least bit fat. She was beautiful. But she claimed if she didn't watch herself, she'd be a tub in no time.

"I'm going to risk it," Elizabeth said, eyeing her sandwich defiantly. "I've got a lot of work to do this afternoon. I'll need the energy."

"That's what they all say," Nina muttered.

After lunch, Elizabeth headed for the library, following Nina's advice and walking as quickly as she could to increase her metabolism. *This is great,* she told herself as she raced across the quad. *Now I'm not hungry, I'm just racked with guilt.*

"Hey, Elizabeth! Slow down, will you?"

Elizabeth turned around. Denise and Anoushka were hurrying toward her.

"You haven't seen Winnie around, have you?" Denise asked when they reached her. "We've been looking for him everywhere."

Elizabeth immediately caught the concern in the other girl's voice. "I haven't seen him in days," she answered. "Why? What's wrong?"

"Denise had a dream," Anoushka said.

"A *dream*? About Winston?" Elizabeth resisted the temptation to smile.

"It was more a premonition," Denise said. She shrugged helplessly. "I woke up this morning convinced that Winnie was in trouble, but when I went to his room to prove to myself that he was all right, he was gone."

Common sense was telling Elizabeth that Denise was upset over nothing, but her own instincts were telling her to pay attention. "He probably had an early class," Elizabeth suggested, hoping to calm both of them.

Denise nodded, but without much conviction. "Look, I know everyone thinks I'm making too big a deal out of this fraternity thing, but last night Winnie told me that he has his last initiation tonight."

"Well, if it's his last initiation, then it's all right, isn't it?" Elizabeth asked. "It's almost all over."

The worried look didn't leave Denise's face. "I'm not so sure about that. I know a couple of other Sigma pledges, and their hazing is all over already. Winnie seems to be the only one still going through it. But when I told him that, he got all quiet and cagey and said it was very secret. He made me promise not to tell anybody that he'd even mentioned it to me."

Elizabeth frowned. "That does sound strange."

"And then I woke up at about three with this really bad feeling," Denise continued. She looked into Elizabeth's eyes. "What do you think, Elizabeth? Why would Winston be the only one still going through it? That's not the way these things usually work."

Anoushka nodded. "All of the fraternities are

pretty much the same, and they've all finished their hazing. None of the Greeks I've asked can figure out why Winnie should be singled out like this."

Elizabeth remembered what Celine had said about the Sigmas' choosing Winston as their special victim, but decided against mentioning this to Denise and Anoushka. Denise, especially, needed to be reassured, not given more to worry about. "At least it'll all be over after tonight," Elizabeth said.

Denise nodded slowly. "I guess you're right. Maybe I'm worrying too much."

"Things will go back to normal after tonight," Anoushka agreed.

Elizabeth stood for a few minutes, watching Denise and Anoushka walk away, her expression thoughtful. It still didn't make any sense. If hazing was over, and they'd made a fool of Winston as they'd intended, why should he have one more initiation to go through?

Elizabeth was standing in front of the full-length mirror on the back of her closet, trying to decide which shirt to wear, when the door suddenly banged open and Celine thumped into the room.

"Don't tell me you're going out *again*," she growled at Elizabeth. "Don't you ever stay in anymore?"

There had been a time when Elizabeth thought that nothing Celine could ever do or say would make her smile, but she'd been wrong. The fact that Celine was upset about Elizabeth's going out again made her want to laugh out loud. "What's the matter with you?" she asked. "I thought you had a heavy date with Peter the Terrible."

"I do." Celine flung herself into her armchair, knocking several skirts and sweaters to the floor. "Only, Mr. Sigma has some fraternity thing to do first." She kicked some of the fallen clothes across the carpet. "Can you believe it? He expects me just to hang around waiting for him because he has something else to do!" Celine sighed dramatically. "Celine Boudreaux isn't used to being treated like this," she announced. "Just who does he think he is? Men usually wait for *me*."

Elizabeth would have started laughing out loud if something Celine said hadn't caught her attention. She watched her roommate in the mirror. "Fraternity thing?" she asked, trying to sound casual. She knew that if Celine thought Elizabeth wanted some information, she wouldn't let her have it. "What kind of fraternity thing?"

Celine kicked off her shoes. "You know what really makes me mad?" she demanded. "Peter's pretending that this is all very last minute, like it's not his fault, but I know this has been planned for ages. I heard him and Bill talking about it last night."

Elizabeth made her voice emotionless and tried again. "So hazing's still going on?" she asked.

"Only for your friend the Egghead," Celine

said, pulling a pack of cigarettes from her pocket. "They have something special lined up for him."

Elizabeth turned around. Warning bells were sounding in her head. She couldn't be bothered to act uninterested now. "Something special? Like what?"

Celine shrugged. "How do I know?" She blew a smoke ring in Elizabeth's direction. "And anyway, even if I did know I wouldn't tell you, would I?"

Elizabeth's urge to wring Celine's neck had never been stronger than it was right now. "Just what do you know, Celine?" she asked, fighting for control.

Celine must have heard the intensity in Elizabeth's voice, because instead of taunting or ignoring her as she usually would, she turned to her. "Don't get yourself all worked up, Princess. It's just boy stuff. You know what they're like." She stubbed her cigarette out in the ashtray beside her. "All I heard Peter say was that there was one final test for the Egg. Then he laughed and said something about Humpty Dumpty."

"Humpty Dumpty?" Elizabeth repeated.

"That's what he said." Celine's eyebrows drew together as she tried to remember. "He thought it was pretty funny that Winston's name should be Egbert and he was going to end up like Humpty Dumpty."

The warning bells were ringing loudly. Elizabeth grabbed her jacket from the closet. "Where is this happening?" she demanded. "Where did Peter go?"

"Don't tell me the Princess is going to the rescue." Celine smirked. "What are you, an overgrown Girl Scout?"

There was no time to argue or to play games. Before she knew what she was doing, Elizabeth had grabbed Celine by the hair. "Just tell me where he is, Celine."

Celine stared back at her, too surprised to move. "I don't know what—"

Elizabeth tugged. "Tell me, Celine. I mean it, or you'll be wearing a wig for the rest of the semester."

Winston looked down. The ground seemed very far away. It almost looked as though it were underwater. *Why is it moving like that?* Winston wondered. *Why is everything so blurred?*

"Stand up, plebe!" someone shouted from below. "You can't just sit there! Stand up."

Winston turned his gaze from the group of small, wobbling figures on the lawn to the half-empty bottle in his hand to the ledge he was sitting on, trying to figure out where he was and what he was doing.

"Sigma house," he mumbled, forcing himself to concentrate. "I'm on the roof of Sigma house." He took another swig from the bottle he was holding. The roof seemed to dip. *But what am I doing here?* Winston wondered. *Why am I on the roof?*

Several of the Sigmas were chanting now. ".Stand up! Stand up! Stand up!"

Winston nodded. That was what he was doing on the roof. He was supposed to stand up. He laughed out loud. How could he have forgotten something so simple and logical? Of course he was supposed to stand up. Winston took another drink, suddenly overcome with a feeling of perfect peace.

If his friends back home could see him now . . . He was going to become a Sigma. He, Winston Egbert, the clown of Sweet Valley High, was going to be one of the big men at Sweet Valley University. Winston grinned and took another slug.

"I'm sitting on top of the world!" Winston shouted. "On top of the world!" He waved to his friends below. The house lurched. Laughter rose up into the night.

"Stand up! Stand up!" they shouted. "You have to stand up!"

He knew that. He was remembering now. He had to stand up and walk from the window he'd climbed out of to the window at the other end of the roof. That was all. Just walk across the ledge and he would be a Sigma forever and ever.

"I'm standing up!" Winston called back. "I'm standing up now." He looked at the bottle. "One more for the road," he told himself, and then laughed. "Except there is no road." He laughed again. "No road, but plenty of whiskey."

"Stand up! Stand up!"

The amber liquid trickled down Winston's chin. Clutching at the window frame, he started to pull himself up. Every time he teetered, the guys on the lawn laughed. "They know I'm not afraid," Winston said. "Lots of guys would be scared right now, but not me."

A cry went up as Winston made it to his feet.

He waved the bottle triumphantly. "I told you I could do it!" he shouted to the people on the ground. "I told you there was nothing to it."

Everyone started to clap.

"All of a sudden, while I was talking to Celine, I had this flash of understanding," Elizabeth said as she steered the Jeep toward the outskirts of the campus where the Sigma house was. "Every year the Sigmas pick a plebe to make a fool of, but it's just a cover. That way, when the time comes that they need someone to sacrifice, no one thinks it's any more than an accident. They just think they went too far."

Tom nodded. "It makes sense, Elizabeth. It definitely makes sense."

"I just wish I'd figured it out a little sooner," Elizabeth said, her face pale and tense. "I just hope we aren't too late."

"Left!" Tom shouted. "There's an empty lot behind the Sigma house. If we go this way, we can drive right into their backyard."

Branches brushed against the side of the Jeep as Elizabeth made a sharp left.

Her heart was racing. "I hope I'm right about this," she said, her knuckles white as she gripped the wheel. She glanced over at Tom. "What if Celine was lying and they're not at the house? What if they've gone somewhere down by the beach, someplace more remote?"

"Then we're in trouble," Tom said. He pointed in front of her. "It's up there on the right," he said. "Just drive through the lot."

"Okay," Elizabeth said, "hold on to your hat." The Jeep jumped the curb, landing with a bounce.

Tom pressed forward, peering through the windshield as they crashed through the tall grass and weeds. "Look!" he shouted, pointing across her. "I see him! You were right, Elizabeth. He's up on the roof."

Elizabeth looked. Winston was standing on the ledge that ran below the second story, his Sigma beanie on his head and what looked like an empty bottle of whiskey in his hand.

"And there's Peter Wilbourne," Elizabeth said as the beams from the headlights cut into the backyard, revealing the laughing circle of Sigmas.

"I think we should let them know we're here," she said as she stepped on the gas.

Several heads turned instantly, their expressions stunned as they watched the Jeep rapidly approaching over the lawn.

Tom leaned over and sounded the horn as Elizabeth pulled to a stop. "Let's let the whole neighborhood know we're here."

Elizabeth threw open her door and jumped from the car. "Winston!" she shouted. "It's me, Elizabeth! Don't move!"

Tom was right beside her. "Keep talking to him, Elizabeth," he said. "I'm going up."

Most of the Sigmas had gotten out of the way when the Jeep screeched to a stop in the middle of the yard. Only Peter Wilbourne and his closest henchmen hadn't budged. Now Peter stepped forward, blocking their way.

"You two aren't going anywhere, Watts." He raised his fist threateningly. "You're on my turf. You'll be polite."

Elizabeth looked from Peter to Tom, fear clenching her stomach. *Please don't let them fight. Not now.*

"Get out of here," Peter commanded. "You take another step and you're history." He and his friends stepped closer, encircling them.

Elizabeth's mind was racing with panic. What could they do? There was no way Tom could take on all of them. She knew how brutal Peter and his henchmen could be.

"Peter, leave him alone," a voice said from behind him.

They all swung around in surprise. Four Sigmas approached, their faces serious. "Look, Peter, we don't want any trouble," one of them said.

Peter's hard face twisted into an expression of outrage.

"A joke's a joke, but this has gone too far," another said. "Let Tom go up if he wants to."

Elizabeth almost cried out with relief.

"You better listen to your friends," Tom advised, roughly shoving the Sigma president aside. "We've already called the cops."

Elizabeth ran past them to the side of the house. "Winston! It's Elizabeth! Don't move, okay?"

"Elizabeth!" Winston shouted. "What are you doing here? The Sigmas don't like you, Elizabeth. You better go home."

"He's drunk," Tom said, coming up behind her. "He can hardly stand."

"Go up," she said, giving him a push. Then, in a louder, calmer voice she called out, "Winston! Just go back to the window. Go to the window and sit down."

Winston waved the bottle in the air. "I can't, Elizabeth. I have to walk across the roof if I want to be a Sigma."

"You're right!" she shouted back, thinking so fast she didn't know what she was going to say until the words were out of her mouth. "That's why you have to go to the window. If you go to the window, you'll be a Sigma. Just go to the window and sit down."

He nodded. "Okay, Elizabeth, if you say so. Okay, that's what I'll do."

Elizabeth held her breath as Winston wobbled along the ledge. Tom appeared at the open window.

Thank God, Elizabeth thought. Thank God she'd had the sense to bring Tom with her.

She could see Tom's lips moving, gently coaxing Winston toward him.

"I'm coming," Winston said as he inched along. "I'm a Sigma now. I can do anything."

Tom held out his hand when Winston reached the window.

"I don't need any help," Winston told him. He held up the bottle. "I'm a big man—I don't need any help."

The bottle slipped from his grasp. Elizabeth watched in horror as Winston grabbed for it and lost his balance, aware that around her everything had gone eerily silent.

Oh God. "Winston!" she whispered.

Just at that instant, Tom lunged forward and pulled Winston inside.

"Let's walk back to campus," Nina suggested. "It's such a beautiful night, and I'm in such a great mood."

"That sounds all right to me, Ms. Harper." Bryan slipped his arm through hers. "I'm in a pretty great mood, too."

Nina smiled up at the moon. She still wasn't accustomed to having such a good time. Rosa MacWilliams, the president of the BSU, had had a pot luck supper in her off-campus apartment, and Nina and Bryan had been invited. Nina knew she was lucky to have been accepted into the heart of the Union so quickly, but she also knew that this acceptance was largely due to Bryan. Bryan was liked and respected by everyone; people took it for granted that he would be the BSU's next president.

"That had to be one of the most fascinating discussions I've ever taken part in," she said to Bryan as they strolled along. "I know you think I'm pretty naive, but I really didn't understand just how much discrimination there still is."

"It's like death and taxes," Bryan said with a wry smile. "It just hangs around, no matter how hard you try to get rid of it." He looked at Nina. "You wouldn't believe the anonymous hate mail and phone calls Rosa gets because of her work for the BSU."

A chill ran through Nina. "It's terrible to think there's so much hatred in the world."

"There's hatred and ignorance on both sides." Bryan's hand wrapped itself around hers as they reached the campus. "That's my mission in life, to somehow try and get rid of at least a little of the hatred and ignorance."

Nina looked at him. He was always surprising her. "I thought you were interested in science."

Bryan laughed. "I *am* interested in science. And playing the blues. And Mexican food. And science fiction. And fighting hatred and ignorance." He stopped suddenly and turned to her. "And I'm interested in you," he said softly. "I'm very interested in you."

"Well, isn't that just lovely? The black boy's very interested in *her*."

Nina, just about to meet Bryan's lips, froze at the sudden intrusion of that harsh male voice. Bryan pulled back, looking around, his whole body tense and alert. Stepping out of the shadows were several men wearing dark clothes and black masks.

"We know what you're interested in, Bryan Nelson," another of the men said with a sneer as the four of them walked slowly toward Nina and Bryan. "You're interested in butting in where you're not wanted."

"Let's go," Nina whispered, tugging at Bryan's hand.

Bryan wouldn't budge. "And what are you interested in, hiding behind your masks?" he demanded. "If you want to talk to me, take off those things and talk like men."

"Bryan," Nina whispered again.

He pushed her behind him. "Run," he hissed under his breath. "I'll stall them as long as I can—just run."

The men came closer, circling Bryan as she backed away.

"Please, Bryan," she moaned. "I'm not going without you."

"Now, Nina! Run!"

The first man moved forward, but Bryan jumped, meeting the masked face with his foot.

Nina screamed as two of the others threw themselves on top of Bryan.

"Run, Nina!" Bryan was still shouting. "Run!"

"No!" Nina screamed. "Leave him alone!" she screamed at the men in masks. She was sobbing as she backed away. How could she leave him like this?

Suddenly someone knocked her to the ground. She no longer had a choice.

"You've had quite a night, haven't you?" asked the young officer who was driving Elizabeth back to the campus. The radio crackled and sent its messages into the night.

Elizabeth sighed. "Yeah, I guess I have." She'd thought everything was over when the police arrived, but in fact things had just begun. First she'd gone to the hospital with Winston, to make sure he was going to be all right, and then she'd been taken to the police station to make a statement.

Officer Davenport turned the car into the campus. "I guess you'll be happy to get back to your dorm."

The familiar lights of the university shone ahead of them. Elizabeth was about to agree that she was going to be more than happy to get back to her dorm when tears suddenly welled up in her throat.

There was something in the sight of the peaceful campus that brought the full impact of the events of the evening home to her like a freight train hitting a wall.

Perhaps taking Elizabeth's silence as shyness, the policewoman glanced over and smiled. "What are you going to do first? Take a bath, eat, or just collapse?"

Elizabeth stared straight ahead at the empty quad, suddenly knowing exactly what she was going to do first. She was hungry, she was tired, and she was emotionally drained, but now that it was all over, and Winston was safe, what she wanted more than anything was to see Tom. The last glimpse she'd had of him was when he was getting into the back of the black-and-white car with its blue light silently flashing.

"Stop here!" Elizabeth shouted suddenly. "Please."

"Here?" Officer Davenport looked at her again. "But this part of campus is nearly deserted. Why don't you let me take you back to your dorm?"

Elizabeth shook her head. "No, it's all right, really. The TV station will be open. I have to meet someone there."

The only light in the room came from a small clip-on light attached to one of the shelves, and the computer screen. Tom was sitting at his desk, already working on the story, just as Elizabeth had known he would be.

She stepped soundlessly into the room, gently closing the door behind her. He was so absorbed he didn't hear her. "Tom?"

At the sound of her voice he turned around. "Elizabeth!" He stood up. Was it relief she saw in his face? "No one would tell me where you were."

For a few seconds, Elizabeth couldn't think of what to say. She was so happy to see him. Somehow, just the sight of him made the horrors of the night seem less real.

"I had to stop by and thank you," she said at last, walking toward him. "You were wonderful. You probably saved Winston's life."

He stood up and faced her, shaking his head. "No, Elizabeth, you saved Winston's life. If you hadn't figured out what was going on . . ."

She came to a stop in front of him, just a few feet away. She felt his intense gaze on her face.

"No, it was you, Tom. Without you—" A few of the tears that had been threatening her in the police car came to her eyes and streamed down her cheeks.

"Elizabeth, what's the matter?" Slowly, Tom stepped forward. With incredible gentleness he put his arms around her and pulled her against him. "Elizabeth, don't cry," he whispered. "Everything's all right now."

"I—" She felt so overwhelmed to be in his arms, to feel her body pressed against his, that she couldn't speak. And even if she could, would he be able to hear her over the pounding of her heart?

As her lips moved toward Tom's it was as though the world had been switched to slow motion; as they touched it was as though the world were standing still.

And then someone turned on the lights.

Elizabeth and Tom jumped apart so quickly, she wasn't sure they really had kissed.

Elizabeth turned. William White was standing in the doorway. She realized in a rush that she'd had a date with him tonight. She'd completely forgotten, but clearly he hadn't. In his hand was a single white rose.

"Celine told me what happened," he said, coming forward. "I've been looking for you everywhere."

Tom gave Elizabeth one last glance filled with uncertainty and anguish before he turned away. "Well, now you've found her."

The dining room table was set for a romantic dinner for two. There were pale purple candles and a yellow orchid in the center of the white linen cloth. On one side of them was a glass bowl filled with salad and on the other, a chicken casserole in a cast iron pot.

But the candles were almost burnt down, the salad was soggy, the casserole was cold, and there was only one person sitting at the table, crumbling bits of wax onto her plate.

Jessica wiped tears from her face, but refused to look at the clock.

"I don't want to know what time it is," she mumbled to herself. "I don't care."

She blew the crumbs of wax across the table. The truth was that she knew what time it was. It was eleven thirty. She'd been home since six. All afternoon she'd told herself that it didn't matter about the Thetas, it didn't matter about having to work in the coffeehouse, it didn't even matter about the redhead yesterday. All that mattered was that she had Mike.

Only, Mike hadn't come home. She'd raced back from campus to fix a special dinner and make herself look especially pretty before Mike got home from work, but he'd never turned up. Seven o'clock came, and seven o'clock went; eight o'clock came and eight o'clock went. At eight thirty she called the garage, but the answering machine was on. At nine o'clock she called the local hospital, in case he'd had an accident. At ten o'clock she started crying. She'd been crying off and on ever since, but no matter how much she wept, there were still more tears. All she had to do was think of him laughing with some other woman, kissing some other woman, and the tears came again.

She should never have insisted on going to the ceremony that night. She should have dropped the Thetas when he first asked her, instead of stubbornly clinging to them. Why had she gone against him like that? Why hadn't she realized what would happen?

"Just come back," Jessica whispered to the empty apartment. "That's all I ask. Just come home, and I'll do whatever you say. I swear I will, just please come home."

The night grew cold around her. The sounds of music and voices coming from other parts of the building echoed in the silence, and the lights from the windows across the way began to go out. Jessica rested her head on her arms and cried some more.

"Baby, what are you doing up?"

Jessica groggily lifted her head from the table. She must have fallen asleep.

"Baby, you don't have any lights on, it's cold . . ."

Jessica blinked. Mike was kneeling beside her. His hair was a mess and his eyes were bleary. She could smell beer; beer and something else, something softer and fruitier, something that could have been perfume.

"Baby . . . baby . . ." he said over and over, stroking her hair. "Baby . . ."

She'd promised herself not to say anything to him, not to be a nag, not to upset him, but somehow the words were out before she could stop them.

"Where were you?" she wailed. "I've been sitting here all night, waiting for you!"

His hands dropped to his sides. His eyes turned cold. "Where was I?" He got unsteadily to his feet. "Why should I tell you where I was?" His voice was quiet but icy.

"I was worried. I—"

Mike's fist hit the table so hard the cutlery jumped. "Worried? Are you trying to tell me that you were worried about me?" He banged the table again. "You weren't worried. You were off with your snotty friends, as usual. Everybody's more important than me." He paced a few steps, his head down, his feet unsteady. "I wanted it to be just you and me, but you're not happy with that. You're just a spoiled brat! You don't care about me!"

"That's not true!" Jessica hurled herself against him. "That's not true, Mike," she sobbed. "You know it's not true. I quit the Thetas, Mike. I quit this afternoon. From now on it will be just you and me."

He looked down at her, the golden eyes as flat as a frozen lake. "Really? You really quit?"

Tears streamed down her cheeks. "Yes, Mike, really. I want it to be just you and me, too. That's all I want, just you and me."

"That's what I want, baby." He pulled her close into the warmth of his body. "And that's the way it's going to be. Always."

SIGN UP FOR THE SWEET VALLEY HIGH® FAN CLUB!

Hey, girls! Get all the gossip on Sweet Valley High's® most popular teenagers when you join our fantastic Fan Club! As a member, you'll get all of this really cool stuff:

- Membership Card with your own personal Fan Club ID number
- A Sweet Valley High® Secret Treasure Box
- Sweet Valley High® Stationery
- Official Fan Club Pencil (for secret note writing!)
- Three Bookmarks
- A "Members Only" Door Hanger
- Two Skeins of J. & P. Coats® Embroidery Floss with flower barrette instruction leaflet
- Two editions of *The Oracle* newsletter
- Plus exclusive Sweet Valley High® product offers, special savings, contests, and much more!

Be the first to find out what Jessica & Elizabeth Wakefield are up to by joining the Sweet Valley High® Fan Club for the one-year membership fee of only $6.25 each for U.S. residents, $8.25 for Canadian residents (U.S. currency). Includes shipping & handling.

Send a check or money order (do not send cash) made payable to "Sweet Valley High® Fan Club" along with this form to:

SWEET VALLEY HIGH® FAN CLUB, BOX 3919-B, SCHAUMBURG, IL 60168-3919

NAME_____
(Please print clearly)

ADDRESS_____

CITY_____ STATE _____ ZIP_____
(Required)

AGE _____ BIRTHDAY_____ /_____ /_____

Offer good while supplies last. Allow 6-8 weeks after check clearance for delivery. Addresses without ZIP codes cannot be honored. Offer good in USA & Canada only. Void where prohibited by law.
©1993 by Francine Pascal   LCI-1383-123

Life after high school gets even *Sweeter!*

Jessica and Elizabeth are now freshmen at Sweet Valley University, where the motto is: Welcome to college — welcome to freedom!

Don't miss any of the books in this fabulous new series.

♥ College Girls #1   0-553-56308-4 $3.50/$4.50 Can.
♥ Love, Lies and   0-553-56306-8
  Jessica Wakefield #2 $3.50/$4.50 Can.
♥ What Your Parents   0-553-56307-6
  Don't Know #3 $3.50/$4.50 Can.
♥ Anything for Love #4   0-553-56311-4 $3.50/$4.50 Can.
♥ A Married Woman #5   0-553-56309-2 $3.50/$4.50 Can.
♥ The Love of Her Life #6   0-553-56310-6 $3.50/$4.50 Can.

Bantam Doubleday Dell
Books for Young Readers

Bantam Doubleday Dell
Dept. SVU 12
2451 South Wolf Road
Des Plaines, IL 60018

Please send the items I have checked above. I am enclosing $_____ (please add $2.50 to cover postage and handling). Send check or money order, no cash or C.O.D.s please.

_____
Name

_____
Address

_____
City   State   Zip
Please allow four to six weeks for delivery.
Prices and availability subject to change without notice.   SVU 12 4/94

Life after high school gets even sweeter!

Jessica and Elizabeth are now freshman at Sweet Valley University, where the motto is: Welcome to college – welcome to freedom!

Don't miss any of the books in this fabulous new series.

♡ College Girls #1 ....56308-4 $3.50/4.50 Can.
♡ Love, Lies and Jessica Wakefield #2........56306-8 $3.50/4.50 Can.

Bantam Doubleday Dell
Books for Young Readers

Bantam Doubleday Dell
Dept. SVH 11
2451 South Wolf Road
Des Plaines, IL 60018

Please send the items I have checked above. I am enclosing $_____ (please add $2.50 to cover postage and handling). Send check or money order, no cash or C.O.D.s please.

Name

Address

City   State   Zip

SVH 11 2/94

Please allow four to six weeks for delivery.
Prices and availability subject to change without notice.

Your friends at Sweet Valley High have had their world turned upside down!

Meet one person with a power so evil, so dangerous, that it could destroy the entire world of Sweet Valley!

A Night to Remember, the book that starts it all, is followed by a six book series filled with romance, drama and suspense.

♡ 29309-5 A NIGHT TO REMEMBER (Magna Edition) ..$3.99/4.99 Can.
♡ 29852-6 THE MORNING AFTER #95...........................$3.50/4.50 Can.
♡ 29853-4 THE ARREST #96..$3.50/4.50 Can.
♡ 29854-2 THE VERDICT #97 ....$3.50/4.50 Can.
♡ 29855-0 THE WEDDING #98..$3.50/4.50 Can.
♡ 29856-9 BEWARE THE BABYSITTER #99....................$3.50/4.50 Can.
♡ 29857-7 THE EVIL TWIN #100 ....$3.99/4.99 Can.

- -

Bantam Doubleday Dell
Books for Young Readers

Bantam Doubleday Dell
BFYR 20
2451 South Wolf Road
Des Plaines, IL 60018

Please send the items I have checked above. I am enclosing
$_____ (please add $2.50 to cover postage and handling).
Send check or money order, no cash or C.O.D.s please.

Name _____

Address _____

City _____ State _____ Zip _____

BFYR 20 1/94

Please allow four to six weeks for delivery.
Prices and availability subject to change without notice.